STORIES FROM A SMALL TOWN GIRL

Stories of life, faith, and laughter

Rebecca Hughes

Rebecca Hughes

Stories from a Small-Town Girl

Stories of life, faith, and laughter

Rebecca Hughes

Published by STE Entertainment LLC

Copyright 2021 STE Entertainment LLC

Edited by Melodie Norris

eBook ISBN: 978-1-7364606-1-0

Cover design by Scott Carpenter

A Note From the Author

For those of you that have encouraged me with kind words as you read my Facebook posts, I want to say, "Thank you". It has only been in the last few years that I have able to put my thoughts down on paper. Before that they mostly hung around in a mind that was unfocused and extremely cluttered. I had no idea that one day God would take all of the clutter in my life and allow me to write it down and someone else might not only read it, but like it. God is like that though. For 60 some years now, I have been on a journey. My journey in life started as the youngest child in a family of six. I know what you're thinking….spoiled….right? Well, maybe a bit, but from that position I was able to view much love, to see how obstacles were overcome, and to learn that life is not always easy, but it should never be taken for granted. I learned from my parents' unconditional love when I told them I was pregnant at 17. I learned compassion for young girls who are raising babies as they are still trying to grow up, because that was me. I have learned that when trials come and life doesn't turn out the way we want, God doesn't leave our side, even though it might seem so at times. So, I am on a new journey. It is one that includes you if you decide to read my stories. And if you want to skip over them that is fine too. But when my mind fills with words that need release….well, they will be poured out in my stories….let the new journey begin.

Thank you to Melodie Norris, my daughter-in-law, who took the time to edit what you are reading. She made sure that my they're, there, and theirs were in the proper sentence, right along with the to, two, and toos. She made sure that what you read was punctuated and spelled correctly. If not for her, this truly would be a real comedy of errors. She is a blessing to me, and even if you don't know it, she is to you too.

Rebecca Hughes

Table of Contents

Life in a Small Town

A JOURNEY BACK

One day my fifteen-year-old granddaughter asked, "Grandma, what do you remember about the time your brother was injured in the war?" and "What was the country like at that time?" She was going to do a speech about her Great Uncle Bruce in school and was in the process of collecting information. As my mind began to remember what my heart had hidden for so long, I prepared my response. I was fifteen years old, the same age as she was, but I was well aware of what was going on in our country in regards to the Vietnam conflict. Protests of the war were being held in most cities and the turmoil in our country was so heavy in the air that when you let yourself breathe it in, it was enough to suffocate you. I had two older brothers, and they were both in Vietnam at the same time: one in the Army and one in the Marines. They had enlisted. Many of the senior boys from our high school were being drafted, as soon as they graduated. Their future had been decided by a group of people in Washington who had sealed their fate. Many would return home to a country that gave them no honor for what they had sacrificed for us. Returning soldiers were spit upon, called names, and treated like lepers. We were a country divided.

As a family we gathered every night around the TV to watch the news... hoping to hear that progress was being made in this war. But instead of hope, what we heard and saw on every channel was more casualties and stories of soldiers being wounded or killed. I would scan the faces of soldiers that were on the news hoping to get a glimpse of one of my brothers and even when I realized that would be almost impossible, I continued to look.

The day we were notified of Bruce's injuries, my brother Dale was home on leave from Vietnam. He watched as a car pulled into the driveway across the street, and two Marines in full dress uniforms got out and went to the door. He knew they were at the wrong address, and they would soon arrive at our house. He also knew it was customary to send out the uniformed Marines if your soldier had been killed. Thankfully, this time was different.

As they made their way to our house, we were all waiting for them. We opened the door, hesitantly, and invited them in. A young man not much older than myself, with the brightest blue eyes, (funny the things you remember) started reading a telegram he was trying to hold still in his hands...but his hands could do nothing but shake. Bruce, my brother, had been injured.

The young Marine continued to shake as he read; Bruce was on his way to a hospital in Japan.

He had lost both of his legs, one arm, and quite possibly his eyesight. My eyes never left the eyes of this young soldier, and as he started to read to us, it was then I noticed tears drop from the corners of his eyes with each sentence he read. The tears came one after another, not a sob, just streaming down his face as he read to us what seemed like a death sentence for my brother.

The dreaded news that all families who have loved ones in a war fear hearing had just been given to us. Oh, we were beyond thankful that our news included a *living* loved one, for we knew many did not. Even with that, each one of us took in that news in our own way, which produced a silence on the outside, but a gasping for air... as it seemed we were drowning on the inside. Our family even in the midst of chaos knew the One who holds us in the storm, and we all screamed silently to Him.

Communication in 1970 consisted of the telephone on the wall. Even with that we were not sure who to call. Someone suggested that we call the Red Cross, and when we did, they were invaluable at getting us information on Bruce. I'm not sure how long he stayed in Japan, a few weeks I think, to stabilize him. What I do remember is seeing the pain in my parents' faces as they longed to see and comfort their son but could not, at least not yet. So, they waited and prayed.

Living in a small community, word got out quickly about Bruce, and that phone on our wall started to ring. Friends and family came to pray with us and also brought us food to eat; their support at this time was indescribable. In the midst of our pain, they brought comfort and God gave us His peace. As it turns out, the telegram was wrong; he did not lose his legs. However, they are filled with shrapnel and still cause much pain today. He did lose eyesight in one eye, and he also lost his left arm just below the elbow...and wouldn't you know it, he was left-handed.

With the trauma he received to his body, mind, and spirit, we knew there would be many challenges and obstacles in his future, but he was ALIVE, and we couldn't wait to see him. Bruce finally arrived in the United States and was taken to the Philadelphia Naval Hospital. We loaded into our car, which I'm sure was a station wagon, with no seat belts, and a bench seat in the back that faced the cars behind us, and we set out to find the hospital three states away. We were all excited about seeing Bruce, but probably all of us a little apprehensive, too.

It was 1970, and travel for the most part was done in the car; there was no way we could afford the luxury of airfare on my parents' income. After many hours on the road, with no GPS, no AAA trip tiks and only a road atlas in hand, we made it safely to Philadelphia, Pennsylvania, from SW Michigan.

The Naval hospital from my memory was huge; it was one of those old brick buildings that are many stories high and straight up; it seemed to extend almost as far as you could see. As we entered the hospital doors that day, our excitement of seeing Bruce must have been written all over our faces. We inquired at the main desk where Bruce was. He was in a ward on the first floor. It was the amputee ward. Going through the doors to this area that day is something even as a fifteen-year-old I knew I would never forget. The sight that was set before me is seared into my mind to this day. We entered the double doors, and there in front of us was a long room with an aisle down the center, and bed after bed all the way down on both sides, filled with only wounded amputee soldiers. Many were in traction; most had several IV's, and all of them seemed to be covered in bandages. But they all had one thing in common. They were now known as amputees. They had lost a part of themselves that could never be replaced. All because they were willing to sacrifice their lives for their country. It still brings tears to my eyes today when I think about it. Heroes, every one of them.

We slowly started our walk down the center aisle. We were staring at each soldier trying to find something familiar on their face. Something that we could recognize, you know, a smile, the look of the eyes, a laugh. It didn't come, and we continued our walk halfway down the aisle. Then a fragile voice from *behind* us said weakly," Mom, Dad...here I am... it's me." How do you put into words, emotions only your heart can feel? Unimaginable joy, overwhelming love, and underlying sadness all rolled into one moment. So, we did walk past him. I think not so much because we didn't recognize him, but because our minds were in the midst of a fog of wounded soldiers and sadness. Each one of them writing a new chapter in their life story, one they never asked for, and one, I am sure, they were all wondering how it would end.

Try as hard as I can, I am unable to come up with my memory of what I did when I first saw my brother. I'm sure there were lots of hugs, (our family is good at hugging). There had to be tears of joy, but most of all thankfulness. I do remember being concerned about what he would look like after all he had been through...but you know what? He looked just like Bruce! Bandages, body cast, and IV's did not change who was lying in that bed. He was my brother. The same one who picked on me nonstop when we were kids, the one who I looked up to and the one who was always full of energy... he was my brother. Maybe his eyes didn't have the same sparkle, maybe his smile wasn't as big as it used to be, maybe his body was wounded, never to be the same again...but I could still see my brother.

His recovery took place over many months. There was unbelievable pain, sprinkled with bouts of sadness and I'm sure some depression, but mostly his days were filled with a determination to do what he had to do to get home...

Home for Bruce is a small town in Michigan, Delton is its name. Months later, he was allowed to come home for the first time. He tells of the time and the feeling he had when he first saw the sign that said "Delton." It was a feeling of belonging, relief, and thankfulness all rolled into one. He knew at that moment; he would never leave the area for very long again. Delton would always be his home. From being severely wounded, thrown in a helicopter, given last rites, and fighting with all he had...he was finally home for good. Bruce had made it, not without trials or frustrations, but with God's help, and a family and community that allowed him to heal and become who he is today in spite of his injuries.

HE WAS HOME!

The rest of my brother's story is played out in the life he continues to live in our community. Most people in our town know Bruce. Even with his injuries, he figured a way to continue to play baseball on the local men's teams. Bruce was impressive to watch, a one-handed ball player...who was a force to be reckoned with. He continues to coach children in several different sports, gives riding lessons as he shares his love for horses with others, has built houses, worked and retired from our school as one of the maintenance crew, owned a General Store, hunts, fishes and snowmobiles and is a great father and husband. I guess you could say there really isn't much that he hasn't tried...and accomplished.

As I watch what he has accomplished and what he has overcome, his zest for life never ceases to amaze me. My brother has never let his injuries keep him from living a full life. There are many stories that could be shared, many successes that have gone unnoticed, but the fact that he gave us his all while in the service and has continued to do so in the way he lives his life is something we should all try to imitate.

Thank you for staying with me on this journey of memories, and if you are wondering...my granddaughter did get an A on her speech.

****

Time Travel?

I know there is no such thing as a time machine, but I swear tonight for just a moment I was transported back in time 50+ years. It happened as I was walking to my car after leaving a friend's house. It could have been the mild crisp autumn air, or maybe it was the sound of the leaves crunching beneath my feet, or was it just the smell of fall all around? I'm not sure exactly what triggered it, but there I was transported back to a memory of 6 kids around a big pile of leaves. Raking until there were no more leaves in sight. We had formed the biggest pile of leaves in our neighborhood...and what else is left to do? Jump!!!.... Leaves covered every inch of each of us and laughter pierced the evening air with delight as it swelled from under the mound. Laughter, Love, Family, Good Memories...Thank You, Lord, for giving me a glimpse of joy on a simple walk to the car.

****

Cemeteries and Kids

As kids growing up, there was nothing special about our daily lives: we did chores, we played, we laughed, and we cried. So why is it that the days of the innocence of my youth are creeping into my mind some sixty years later? My mind is being filled with many scenes that were played out in my childhood. Oh, to go back to the days gone by.

Growing up in Prairieville with six siblings in a town filled with kids brought much laughter, mischief and adventure. Living almost directly across from the cemetery was something I considered pretty cool. Yes, we sometimes made it a place to play. We rode bikes on the roads that weaved in and around the graves. We took time and checked out names on some of the stones. We would look for the oldest stone or the biggest one…and of course there would always be a stop at the stone of the dog. Oh, and we would wonder about that dog. As the story goes, the dog's master had died and the dog would not eat or leave the grave of his master. He died in the cemetery by his master's grave. A stone was ordered identical to the dog and he is still there as he continues to guard his master at least 100 years later. At the time we didn't know if the story was true, but it sure made for much discussion about our dogs. We were all sure that our dogs would die in order to be with us, too…thankfully we never had to find out.

With lots of kids in our family it usually meant that a friend might be staying over on any given day. So, it was the day that my sister had her friend over. Not being that much younger than my sister, Pat, when either of us had friends over, all of us would hang out together. On one specific night Julie was over and of course, Pat and I were telling tall tales about the cemetery. The story would start out with us saying "If you went to the cemetery at a certain time…as soon as you would walk through the gates and enter in…. the wind would start to blow, letting you know you were not welcome." Well, this friend wanted to go and check it out. We obliged. It was dark, no flashlights, no cell phones, only three young girls with our arms locked together for the walk of fear. Knowing there was no such thing as the wind blowing on the entrance to the cemetery, we wondered just how we were going to explain it to our friend when it didn't happen. As we approached the entrance that dark night…. you guessed it….at the moment we were to go in….the wind did come up as we walked in….and three young girls, as fast as they could, hightailed it back to our house, with a few screams, our hearts pounding and laughter abounding. We made it back home. We were safe.

As much fun as we had playing in the cemetery, I also remember watching from our living room window many funeral processions. Long lines of cars would turn in behind the hearse carrying a deceased loved one. I knew there was sadness in the loss of a family member. I knew you stayed away from the cemetery when a funeral was taking place, and I learned how grief can overcome you from watching a mom whose daughter had died from a childhood illness. I remember watching this mom as she made a daily trip to the cemetery. I knew her car. I knew exactly where she went, and I knew her heart was broken even at my young age. Day after day, year after year, I really am not sure how long it went on, but I remembered wondering what she did when she was there. She never stayed long, but she never missed a day. I have to wonder if her heart ever healed from that loss. I hope she found her joy in life again. I will probably never know. But she taught me at a very young age that loss is inevitable, love never ends, and that while cemeteries hold our loved one's bodies, we get to hold their memories.

****

May 22, 2017

Twenty-two years ago today, the world lost a great man who I was blessed to call Dad. Many of you never knew my father. He was always full of laughter. I can still hear him singing silly songs around our house that would fill the air with joy. Hearing him sing special music in church would make my heart swell with pride, although I'm sure I never told him. He was a World War 2 veteran but never spoke much about the horrors of the war he witnessed. He chose to look on the brighter side of life. Was he a perfect man? Absolutely not! Was he the perfect man to father all six of us kids? ABSOLUTELY! I can see so many of my father's traits in each one of us, that when we are together, well, it's like he's right there with us. So, Dad, we will continue to strive to be more like you, pointing others to our Heavenly Father. Can't wait for the day when we see you again. I miss you, Dad.

****

Here it is, Christmas Eve 2018.

I can hardly believe we will be saying goodbye soon to another year. Today has been about putting the finishing touch on those few things that were put off earlier. I delivered a few last-minute gifts, set our table for tomorrow, and put a turkey in the roaster. I think all of the things on my "to-do" list for today are finished. It's a good feeling.

Family will be here in the afternoon tomorrow, and inside these walls that I call home there will be

laughter, loud talking, gifts and of course lots of food. Our physical bodies will have all we need.

But we are not just physical beings. So tonight, I will attend a candlelight service and prepare for

the spiritual gift that has been given to all of us. Just as I take much time and care preparing for

my physical needs, I need to also prepare for the best gift ever. So tonight, I will focus on the best gift of all. Jesus. He is a Light for a dark world, a Peacemaker in your chaos, and a Savior for all.

May your heart be filled with His joy. Merry Christmas!

And just like that...Christmas 2018 is over.

At our house it will be remembered for the flu bug that managed to work its way through our family. Two family members stayed away from the festivities because of it and four were here but still recovering from it. We managed to pack away lots of yummy food, laughed at crazy gifts received, but we missed those not able to be with us. The empty spot in our family was evident to all of us. Then I stopped and realized so many of you are celebrating with gaping holes in your heart. You have places at your table that will never be filled again...your heart breaks on the inside as you smile on the outside. I hope each of us will see our loved ones for just how precious they are. We all know that none of us are promised tomorrow.... we must learn to love TODAY!

****

What is going on in the world?

Sometimes I just get the feeling I should write something. Most times I have no clue what to write, it's just an urge to empty the thoughts that run through my mind. Today I have that urging. I am extremely disappointed in parents that would choose to buy their children's entrance to a certain college...oh integrity, where have you gone? I hear of police officers being shot. Oh, respect for authority, where are you? People who wrong others and get away with it...oh...Justice ...where are you hiding? Is there anything in this world that is going right? Compassion, caring, selfless actions, where are you? Do you still exist in this selfish world? The answer is yes.... they are seen in the small acts of kindness that each one of us can be a part of. Making this world a better place starts with you...and me. I can't begin to change someone else, but I can change me! I pray that God would use each of us to make a difference in the lives around us...I hope you will join me in that prayer!!! And then maybe soon our society will again find those important things we have lost.

****

The General Store

On my Facebook page this morning there was a picture of the store in Prairieville. I can't begin to tell you all the memories that picture brought to mind. When I was a little girl growing up in Prairieville, the store was the best place to go. The penny candy section was to die for. With five cents you could easily fill a small bag...some pieces were two for a penny! Walking to the store was almost a privilege. I would pick up items for my mom and I could even buy my dad a pack of cigarettes. My, times have changed, haven't they? If that store could talk it would tell a story of a town that knew everyone and a town that truly cared about each other. Where the kids all played together, families worshiped together and where growing up was just fun! It is with gladness and laughter that I can say I grew up in the town of Prairieville...the memories that were made there will last me a lifetime.

****

Birthdays and Sons

Tomorrow will mark another milestone in my life. It's not my birthday, but it was the day I entered the grand profession of motherhood several years ago. Steve, I won't say how old you are because that would date me too. To be honest with you though, I can't think of a time that I regretted having children young. Oh, I made many mistakes along the way because trying to raise children while still a child was hard. But that time goes by in an instant....and before you know it, you are face to face with an adult son, who you admire, respect and love with your whole being. You see what an awesome and godly father and husband he is, but you never ever lose sight of that little boy who gave you hugs, brought you insects to share in one hand while holding a dandelion in the other. Motherhood slips out of our hands while we are busy planning for the future. I guess what I am trying to say to parents out there...stop and enjoy those little ones, enjoy the frustrations, enjoy the smiles, but most of all realize that the little face you are looking at will soon be an adult that you had a part in molding... Relax and enjoy the ride. And Steve, Happy Birthday one day early...you are an awesome son.

****

Cemeteries and Grandkids

Today was the last Monday I would be watching my grandsons before school starts. Of course, I had something special planned. With me, "special" is going to be... let's say "different." We went to the Prairieville Cemetery. Yes, the cemetery! I grew up across the street from the cemetery and walking through it now is like walking through my childhood. I wanted to show them my dad's grave. We talked about who he was, and how I miss him even 25 years after his death. I explained to them that he knew Jesus, so without a doubt I would see him again. And someday, they would meet him too. They just have to make sure they know Jesus. I walked with them through the graves and shared with them stories of my past. Hazel Bagley made the best popcorn balls, and her husband George was the nice man who owned the garage. We saw a stone of my 3rd-grade teacher and a grave that holds one of my best friends. I told stories of the names on many of the stones. They needed to be reminded that the people in the graves were alive at one time too, just like them. We walked over and saw the dog stone, and I shared the

23

story with them about the dog. I showed them the stone I would sit on when I was a kid, and sometimes even did my homework there. (You were never interrupted and it was always quiet.) We noticed graves of those who fought in the wars, we read names and dates of birth and death and we wondered how some had died so young. Yes, there was some sadness; memories of loved ones who have died can do that to us. But there was also laughter. In this crazy world now, we certainly need that, don't we? After getting home, my youngest grandson said to me, "Grandma, when you die, I will bring my kids to see you and tell them all about you, and I will read them Bible stories every day." What could make a day any better?

****

Motherhood

Forty-four years ago today, at the age of seventeen, I became a mother. At the time I was sure I knew everything about raising children. I did a lot of babysitting and really liked kids, so what's so hard about a baby? As I was leaving the hospital with a beautiful little boy…fear set in. How in the world could I begin to know anything about being responsible for this new life that had been entrusted to me? I loved my little boy and his brother that came two years later. We laughed, we cried, we played, we enjoyed life. As I look back, the one thing I did not realize then, but know for a fact now…is what a true gift from God my children were. I think if I had realized it then, maybe I would have loved more deeply, would have hugged longer, and would have thanked God more. We can never go back, so I write this for those new moms who are just starting out. Thank God for the life He entrusted to you. Don't take one day for granted, spend every minute you can with them…they are the reason you have for living. So, Happy Birthday Steven, you survived a 17-year-old mom…I couldn't be prouder of the godly man you are.

****

Grandmas and Grandpas

There are moments in our lives that we can look back and pinpoint a time that changed us. Something that has caused us to sit back in awe and wonder why we deserve such a blessing. I have had many of these times in my life; I am sure you have too. They are what I call the icing added to our cake of "Life!" Nineteen years ago today

24

was one of those times for me. My "Life on the Gray Side" didn't start then, but it made me look face to face with the fact that my life was now in a new era. I became a Grandma. This was a new role for me, one that you don't practice for, one where there are no directions, and one that I couldn't wait to take part in. A new life that I didn't have to be responsible for, but one that I got to share in all the blessings and joy that children bring. Today, Abigail is 19 years old. I so wish I could go back and have one more tea party with you, one more time of dress up, and one more story to read, but those days are a cherished memory, only to be played out in the field of "what used to be." So, today I am thankful for the blessing of you, Abby. You are kind, you are beautiful inside and out, and your life is really just beginning as you step into the plan that God prepared for you 19 years ago. I know you will have a Happy Birthday and I know you will enjoy your day. I just wish we could go back and have another tea party where Grandpa waited on us and laughter was served as the main course.

****

A trip to the Polls, November, 2020

If you haven't realized it yet...today is voting day in America. In the process of waiting in line to cast my vote, I was joined by several people in our township who were doing the same thing. The line was long, the sun was out, and guess what… I heard laughter. There was no sign of discourse...no sign of arguing...no sign of unrest. There was laughter, and that is what caught my attention. Even though I am sure both parties were represented in the line and voting for each of us was obviously important...but it gave way to what this country is all about. It's us! Your neighbors, your family and your friends. My heart was blessed as I waited in the voting line today. For today I saw many take our voting privilege seriously, which sad to say has not been evident in the past. I have hope for our country, not because of who is running, but because today I saw the American spirit as I waited in line to vote. Hope you do the same...

****

Remembering Grandparents

It seems to me that living "Life on the Gray Side," not only has you forgetting what you walked into the kitchen for, but it also puts memories in your mind that you thought were buried forever. I don't know why the memory of the trips to my grandparents is lingering in the chambers of my mind...but before I forget it... I am going to share it. Both sets of my grandparents lived in the Kalkaska area. I saw my grandparents maybe twice a year. The trip was long...and I remember trying to find anything to do that would stop me from asking my parents for the hundredth time... "Are we there yet?" I counted the bridges we would go under, now known as overpasses; I would hold my breath as we would pass a cemetery...the one in Mt Pleasant seemed to never end; and of course, we always stopped at a roadside picnic table to have a ground bologna sandwich and a cookie that my mom had packed for the trip. Do you remember when picnic tables would dot the countryside for a family to get a quick break from their travels?

It seemed like forever before we would finally arrive at my grandparent's house. As we stepped out of the car, we stepped into a different life. My grandparents had an outside toilet, they had no running water inside and no kitchen sinks to wash dishes, only metal tubs that would come out and be placed on a small counter in preparation for the dishes we would use. Water was pumped from the well behind the house; yes, I have gone to a well to fetch water. Yes, I have used an outhouse, though many times at night when nature called, I would step out the back door and squat...Sorry Grandma, but I was too scared to go all the way to the outhouse by myself. Memories of eggs for breakfast that would float on top of 6 inches of lard as they cooked, along with a portion of spam for all. I'm not sure why, but I also remember having cake for breakfast. Sleeping upstairs, under a pile of quilts so heavy that once you got into bed there was no way to move. My Grandma Webb I am sure was the forerunner of the weighted blankets of today. It was different there at my grandparent's house in the country; they lived a quiet life. I remember Grandpa listening to the Detroit Tigers on his radio, (they did not own a TV), taking a walk every morning, reading his Bible and chewing his tobacco; Grandma playing piano, cooking, and sewing...and giving me a lifetime of love for no-bake cookies. Life was simple for them; they had all that they needed, they never complained, kept to themselves and lived the life they were placed in with grace. Thanks Grandpa and Grandma Webb, even in your quietness you spoke volumes to me. Next memory...My Grandma Campbell who lived in the big town of Kalkaska, Mi.

****

Remembering Grandparents (Part 2)

After a nice walk with my sister Sandy in the Prairieville Cemetery today, I was able to talk with her about her memories when we would stay at my Grandma's house in Kalkaska. Just as we stepped into another world when we went to our grandparents in the country, we also opened a door to a much different place as we arrived at my grandmother's house in Kalkaska. My grandfather had died when I was just a baby. Their home then was on a large farm that my grandmother could no longer take care of, so she purchased a small house almost in my aunt and uncle's backyard. It was a big plus for us since my cousins Janice and Terry were always there to show us the ropes of town living. Upon entering my Grandma Campbell's house, you were greeted with a big hug. Now my grandma was maybe 5 ft tall, and quite round... (I remember soft). Her hair was always in a bun on top of her head, only taken down at night when she slept. I don't know if she ever had her hair cut. (Any cousins out there remember if she did?) Her hugs drew you in, her generous smile let you know you were loved, and her laughter filled the air letting you know that you were going to enjoy your week. And we did. She let us go and get her mail, which was several blocks away; she let us buy candy at the local store, and she let us roam most of the day doing nothing except getting to know her and our cousins. Even though my grandparents were as different as night and day, they both helped me see that love is found not in the beauty of the home, it is not found in all the extra things that we think we have to provide for our children, love is found in the soul. It spills out from you, whether you are quiet or outgoing, and it pours out on those who have your heart. My grandparents had my heart, and they poured their soul out on me. I will be ever thankful for the love that came from them. It was different in the way they expressed it, but I just knew it was there. My hope is that my grandkids will remember me with squishy hugs, lots of laughter and of course...great desserts! Right along with knowing that with Jesus, the best is yet to come.

****

A note from a gravestone

Since tonight we set our clocks ahead, I am taking this morning to make sure I am ready to meet the time change with courage. You guessed it; I am enjoying a relaxing morning at our cottage. There is something that is calming as I watch the sun streaming through my still dirty windows, sipping a cup of coffee with the news on in the background, and knowing that I can enjoy this comfy housecoat I am wrapped in... at least for a little while yet. It really is an almost perfect morning. I reach for the Bible that was gracing my coffee table and as I open it...a small slip of paper floats to the ground. Grabbing it off the floor and reading the words written on it, I smiled. I realized that it was something I had jotted down from a cemetery grave in Kalkaska, Michigan. Both sets of my grandparents were laid to rest there, and from my childhood days, I have been, should I say... drawn to cemeteries. So of course, I scouted out the graves around my grandparents. I came upon a stone several years ago that had these words written on them. Words that resonated in my soul. "Remember me as you pass by, as you are now, so once was I, as I am now, you soon shall be...so prepare you now to follow me." Thought-provoking for sure. Enjoy your day...and don't forget to set your clocks ahead!

****

Valentines cookies

Can someone please help me figure out what these conversation hearts mean? For years I have made Valentine's cookies for my grandkids...nothing fancy...a frosted sugar cookie with a candy heart that says...I Love You. I have to admit I was not sure what message I was putting on the cookies this year. In the past things like "be mine," "I love you," or "crazy bout you," adorned the hearts. But what the heck is"dm me?" or "bae?" or "yaaas?" The one that stood out to me the most was "goat!!!" Really...goat? I have no clue what hidden secret saying I placed on top of my cookies this year, do you? Help...I'm a grandma in my 60's trying to keep up with today's slang...I am pretty sure I am failing at it!!!

****

Valentine's Day

When I was growing up Valentine's Day was the culmination of a week of making cards, cutting them out, writing something special on them, and secretly placing them in a box to be handed out on Valentine's Day. I loved making cutout hearts, it's still about the only crafty thing I can make, but the memory of that time still conjures up a heart of love. And today isn't it all about love? Love is displayed in many ways. Oh sure, candy, flowers, and candlelight dinners are great, but with age I am becoming so much more aware of a different kind of love. It is the love that seeks to serve, to share and to care for others instead of you. What is the most loving gift given to you? Out of the many that I have been given there is one that stands out.

I was working every day, and it was a very cold Michigan winter morning. I knew that my car was on empty, and I knew that I would need to fill it before going to work. That meant cold hands, cold face, windy blowing snow, and also having to leave my house a bit early. I was not looking forward to the task. But that morning, before I went to work, without knowing it, my husband took my car and filled it and said nothing...what a gift. He knew how to do...love in action! Gifts don't always come wrapped with a bow.

****

Mini Class Reunions

This past Monday I met up again with a group of women which one of the things we have in common is the school we attended.... many years ago. I think it has been about a year now that we have been getting together every few months. It's funny how time changes things; I remember at graduation thinking I couldn't wait to get out of that school and start being an adult. I just wanted out. Of course, not moving out of Delton I continued to see some classmates in passing and hearing about others and where they had landed in life. Seems now though we have almost come full circle, back to the place where life was so much simpler. We can now put aside those groups we were placed in and appreciate the diversity each of us brings to this much wiser group. We have retired teachers, nurses, factory workers, counselors and mission coordinators right alongside artists, caregivers, and good cooks. We are quite the crew. Each time we meet it seems we add one or two more classmates. We are sharing life together again, only this time it's not about prom dates and homework, it is about the difficulties of caring for our elderly parents, or sharing the joys of our grandkids, and giving comfort to those who have experienced the loss of loved ones. Each one of these girls from school, even though I didn't realize it then, had a part in making me who I am today. So, I look forward to the next time where laughter comes easy, where gray hair and conversations flow...and where the girls from the '70s are still pretty cool!

****

Estate Sales and Tickets

Yesterday as I was going to town to do some banking, I saw an Estate Sale sign TODAY. For those of you who know me well, you know that this invokes in me a challenge. My mind starts to process many questions. Do I have enough time to stop? How far away is it? What should I be looking for? I reason with myself, " You don't need anything, do I have extra cash?" and all of this is going on in my mind in seconds...then right up ahead...there it is, cars parked all along the road...I have to do it! I stop. I know I am a garage sale junkie. This one might have that one kitchen gadget I don't have, or maybe a piece of furniture I have no room for, I will never know unless I stop. The sale was on a corner lot, so in my excitement to get my car parked I followed the crowd. I parked behind a long line of cars on the side street. Hurrying into the sale I felt like a soldier going into battle and I was going to conquer this sale. And I did. I found this one item for 25 cents. Yes, 25 cents. I was a happy shopper. Walking back to my car, I found it strange mine was the only one left on the side street. I didn't think I had stayed that long, but that's when I noticed it...a pretty yellow piece of paper held on by my windshield wiper. Yes, today as I sit and look at my 25 cent estate sale item, I am also writing out a $10.00 parking ticket. So, I did learn a couple lessons...don't always follow the crowd when parking, and don't try to stop at a sale without my sister Sandy Kirk...she would have made sure we parked in the right spot and if not, she would have shared the ticket with me.... right, Sandy?

****

Tomorrow is Halloween.

I remember it not only as a day, but a month-long event. I am pretty sure we started to plan our costumes as soon as the calendar flipped from September to October. Our family never made a trip to the store to buy a costume. With six kids we could not have afforded such luxury. We had to create our own. So, the first thing on our agenda would be to decide what or who we wanted to be, then set out on the task of making our idea turn into a reality. We could be anything we wanted, but it seems my brothers would always end up being cowboys, and for some reason my sister and I would always be hobos. None of that princess stuff for us. Does anyone today even know what a hobo is? Our hobo costume would include a shirt of my dad's, and his pants too, a belt to keep them up and a pillow under the shirt, I guess to make us look older. To accent the costume, you would find a stick you could place over your shoulder with a bag, (a shirt) tied on the end. We probably used some coal to darken spots on our faces, just to make us look a bit tattered. There we were two girls transformed into the best costume our imagination could afford. We rocked it. With our pillowcase in hand, (no special bucket) we set out for the best trick or treat spot ever.... (or at least we thought so) Prairieville. We would walk from house to house. Up one side of the street, and down the other. Knocking on each door, yelling "trick or treat"...to be greeted by our neighbors who knew us, but pretended they didn't. No one was scared, no one worried about getting bad candy. It was just fun. I think there is much to be said about a time where innocence and community walked hand in hand. A time where you could think you looked like a million bucks in a costume from your dad's closet.

Oh, those truly were the days...

****

(Our local school each year hosts a Veterans Day Program, and each year I am moved by the meaning, content and the chance to say thank you to our local heroes. I am honored to write about them.)

November 2019

The Delton Kellogg School pulled off another great Veterans Day Program. Each year they seem to outdo themselves, and this year was no exception. How can you not be moved to tears when you are surrounded by so many that gave their all for this country and then returned home and continue to give their all to the community? There is camaraderie and a respect for each other that is obvious in the Veterans as they interact with each other. They are a group of men and women who are and have been a part of something much bigger than themselves. They were trained to follow orders, they were willing to sacrifice their lives, and they are heroes, each of them. Today there were a couple of Veterans in attendance from WW2, and as they stood slowly from their chairs to be honored, the crowd could not remain in their seats either. As their applause echoed through-out the gym, my heart swelled with pride. This was the group my father would have stood in, humbling for sure. The speaker was an inspiration as she told of her story as a farm girl from outside of Plainwell. She enlisted and was assigned to the Army band playing French Horn, and then was reassigned as a sharpshooter protecting 5 of our Presidents over a 25-year span. The kids always do a great job; they are respectful and quiet during the program. The band, the singers...well, what can I say? It's just another great reason to live in Delton, where we honor those who have served. Thank you again Delton Kellogg Schools, for providing us a way to say thank you to our Veterans.

****

Today I was once again drawn to the Veterans Day Program at the Delton School. This is probably the fourth one I have attended. I am not sure how they do it, but each year they manage to well tears in my eyes. As I watched from the bleachers, each military branch was honored, and my hands could not be stilled as they clapped in honor of the men and women who have served our country from our community. Faces of courage, hearts of selflessness, and pride in their country was evident as they each stood when their branch of service was honored. Children stilled to a silence as the flags entered, carried by retired soldiers. Songs that gave all of us an undeniable pride in our country, and a "Welcome Home" with thanks to our Vietnam vets were just slices of this tribute. I found myself realizing just how blessed I am to live in Delton. To live and do life with heroes every day is something I hope we never take for granted. Thank you, Delton Kellogg Schools, for this very important reminder.

****

Veterans Day

This morning I have loved scanning the pictures of the Veterans in your families as you give them the honor they so deserve. I, too, have many family members who have served in the past and a nephew who is still serving. What I realized this morning, and I hope right along with all of you, is that we live in freedom because of the willingness of those all around us who gave up the everyday life that we call normal...to be set apart and do what is not normal. They leave their families for long periods of time so I can be with mine. They learn to fight so I can live in peace; they learn to lay down their lives for others so I can live. They truly embody what it means to love. Not a fleeting feeling of this world, but one out of this world. John 15:13: "Greater love has no man than this, that he lay down his life for a friend." Today, I can say I have been blessed to live among many of them, my dad, my father-in-law, my uncles, my brothers, and my brother-in-law. So today, I join each of you in giving thanks to our veterans. They deserve our respect, our honor, and our utmost gratitude.

****

November 2020 (the year of Covid)

Tomorrow is Veterans Day. I am sad there will not be a Veterans Day program at the school this year. There is something so special about being in the midst of our local heroes, watching as our community honors those who gave so much for our country. I will miss the children singing songs of patriotism and the flags being brought in as we would all stand in respect. I will miss each soldier as they rise from their seat as the song that represented their branch of service is being played by the high school band. I will miss the feeling of pride in our neighbors, family and friends as they would come to say thank you for all of your sacrifices. So much honor, so much courage, so much selflessness that it seemed one room could hardly contain it. I am going to miss saying thank you in person to those who served, but I will never forget your service. You truly are the hidden heroes in our town. We are all better because of you. Thank you.

****

D-Day

I decided to watch a documentary tonight on D-day. The program consisted of what Normandy looks like today, how we invaded the different beach areas, and it also had interviews of soldiers who took part in the actual invasion of Normandy. Listening to stories of their courage, bravery and valor was overwhelming. Soldiers, young and old, lost their lives immediately after stepping onto the beach, and yet, they never gave up. This was the generation my dad came from. I remember a few talks with my dad about his time in the war; it was something he didn't dwell on. Or he kept it inside, never letting his family in on the horrors of his memories. For tonight though, I can't seem to get out of my mind the thousands of white crosses that mark the graves of American soldiers in France. It is truly a field of honor, a field of heroes, and a field filled with America's best. We must never forget what they did for us!

****

Some things are too hard to watch.

Do you know that nauseating feeling that comes from watching something that your mind just can't comprehend? I have always been intrigued with WW2 and the Nazi takeover. Today I started to watch a film that was taken when the death camps were liberated. I say "started" because I could not finish it. The film left pictures in my mind too vivid and horrific to imagine. Bags filled with women's hair, mounds of eyeglasses, shoes and humans. No difference shown between a pair of glasses and human remains.

I have wondered how depraved a person must be to take part in such madness, and yet the neighbors that were marched through the camps to see firsthand the evil that took place in their own backyard seemed eerily like normal people. Did they just look the other way? Did they go inside when the furnace started up? Did they just live their lives as normal since it didn't really affect them? Questions I must ask myself, what would I do? Will it ever happen again to a people group? God forbid. Help me Lord to always see the value you place on Human Life. I will finish the film.... just can't do it today. My heart is too heavy.

****

Horror of War

I spent the morning with my brother and my sister over coffee, knowing I wanted to tell my brother on Veterans Day "Thank you" for his service to our country. In the process of our conversation, stories of his time in Vietnam came to the surface. I am still trying to process all that he went through as a 19year-old. From the innocence of a young soldier to the realization of the horrors of war, he spoke, retelling the stories of courage, fear, death, and divine intervention. As he shared with us unspeakable things that he kept hidden for years, my heart broke. That he has been able to carry on a normal life and continue to be a blessing to others is nothing short of a miracle. I thank God that He allowed both of my brothers to come home safely from Vietnam. I salute both of them. I am honored to be called their little sister. If any one of you today sees Dale or Bruce Campbell, tell them thanks. Behind the smiles we often don't realize what they have been through.

****

A House Museum

It's interesting that all of a sudden in my Facebook feed I am being bombarded by ads that want to tell me how to make my house have the "Modern Look." You know, they show you what you absolutely should not have in your home if you are going to be "in style." So of course, it got the best of me, and I clicked on the site to find out how this would work in my home. First off, my gold trimmed shower stall has to go! No one has those anymore. Next, the linoleum in my kitchen is too 90's, and must be removed. Of course, the wall to wall carpet in my living room is from the dark ages. Oh, shelves on your walls are so not cool, doilies on your end tables...what century were you born in? The oak cupboards and kitchen table...what are you thinking? So, I have been pondering my dilemma and I think I have come up with a win-win solution. Today...my house becomes a museum...open to the public on Mondays and Fridays. For a fee of just $15 you will be able to get a glimpse of a real-life experience of a working home from the darkest ages. Yes, you will tour a dated bathroom, you will see a grandmother- made doily on an end table, a father's handmade shelf on a wall and you will be invited to have coffee from a real coffee pot, while you sit and enjoy the company of the owner at her oak table!

Opening soon...but not for the faint of heart.

****

July 2019 Conquering the Secretary of State's Office...and winning...I think!

Today I got a glimpse of what people feel like when they have won a well-earned award. It started this morning on an uneventful trip to the Secretary of State. Paul and I set out to get his license renewed, and to do a few other things that we could not do online. We arrived quite early, around 9:30, and took our number. The plan was clearly laid out for us: get the number, get a seat, and wait. The screen showing the number said 99. We were 34 (after 100 they start back at 0 again). There were 3 very efficient women behind the counter calling out numbers and doing what needed to be done. We waited. And we waited. After about an hour of waiting, they were on number 10. Looking around the room, everyone seemed to be very patient. There was a line of people seated in the back who were laughing and joking about how long it was taking. Some were reading; most were like Paul and me, who sat and stared at the number on the wall and waited. Another hour.... a few more people were called up and we waited. I could feel our excitement build when the screen hit #30. Pretty soon we would hear #34: "Come on down!" It was really going to happen. Our number was only 4 people away.......I quickly scanned the room for those people that show up in the return line, no one there...number 33 was called. This was it, our time of receiving the award.   We stood....and we weren't called. Someone had just walked in and was standing in the return line and of course, they were being called before us. Feeling defeated, we sat down, and the crowd around us sighed, sensing our pain. But then we heard it: #34. We bounded from our chairs. I wanted to bow and wave and say thanks to everyone there for making this happen as we made our way to the counter...yes, we had made it. It was our turn. Too bad for those who were still seated...this was our moment. When we approached the desk I thought we should have been given something special.... a high five from the lady behind the counter, a t-shirt that said "I survived the SOS office" or how about a sticker that said "I didn't lose my marbles at the SOS office today". Well, we received nothing; in fact, we had to pay $116 dollars for that experience. But for just one brief moment, I felt that exhilarating feeling that comes with winning the prize...but it ended so quickly. As we were leaving, 3 hours after we had arrived, I caught a glimpse of the couple that had been seated next to us, and I wondered how long they would be there. Their number was 81; they are probably calling out for pizza now and getting ready to inflate the mattress they brought. Yup...pretty sure they are spending the night. Oh, what a morning it was.

****

Why I love Michigan.

A few months back I was sitting on my couch, wrapped in a cozy blanket, peering out at the below freezing cold view outside of my window, asking myself, "Why do I live in Michigan?" Fast forward to July 20: I am sitting on the same couch, 90+degrees, no electricity, and I ask myself again, "Why do I live in Michigan?" And my inner reply is easy, #1----My family is here, #2---My family is here, #3---Where else can I live that the weather gives me exactly what I long for? Winter months, I long for warm summer breezes; on hot summer days, I long for cooler days and bonfires. Michigan gives me what I want, just not when I want it. Aw, Michigan, the land of great mood swings. I hope you swing back a bit. Not all the way to freezing cold yet.... but just to the point where breathing is easier, where no air conditioning is needed, and where my electricity can resume what it does best...make me a happy girl.

****

November 2020

This morning I was notified that a friend I have known since our school days was tragically killed in an auto accident along with her husband and his mother. My heart has been sad all day. I have been trying to make sense of this and I can't...it just isn't fair...So today I have been pondering the fact that yesterday morning when Sharon M. got up, she didn't know it was going to be her last day here. When she posted on her Facebook that morning, she had no clue it would be her last voice to us. When she got into her car that day, she never realized it would be her last ride...and neither do we. Every time this happens, I tell myself to make my days count, to

37

make sure my family and friends know how much I love them, to appreciate each day that I am gifted and not waste it or take advantage of it. So today I am telling myself this over and over...because you know...tomorrow is not a for sure thing. Praying for this family in their loss.

****

A First...Caskets, Laughter and Family

Today I experienced a first. Now at 65 you don't get too many firsts, and I can say I really did enjoy it...in spite of what we were doing. I had an appointment to meet with my mom and my sister at the local funeral home. My mom just turned 90 years old and she decided to get her funeral plans done. My interactions with a funeral home up until now have been after a death, when you are broken hearted, sad, and mostly in a fog. Well, today that changed. Okay, it was a bit strained at first, just how are you supposed to react as you look through a book of caskets? Ummm...we laughed! As my mom was concerned about just how she was going to fit in it, I was wondering if they offer memory foam, and my sister Sandy was concerned about everything matching.....and we laughed some more. But she picked one, and a vault, which you need, but no one ever sees it...and you have the choice of having the vault with holes on the side or solid. She picked solid...the holes just seemed strange to her. We talked about where she wanted her funeral, what she wanted as far as music and which Pastor would do her service. All during this time, there was laughter. Most of you probably think we're strange, heck most of the time we think so too...but the laughter was there because we know that when my mom's body will one day be placed in the casket, she picked out today, and she is placed in the ground, we know without one doubt she will be home in heaven with Jesus.

And so today, we laughed at death, because we know death here means eternal life with Christ...because of His death on a cross for us! So, I can say even in doing the difficult...it really was a pretty fun day.

****

Father's Day

I am already seeing pictures of the special fathers in your lives. They bring a smile to my face as I think back to my dad. Nothing special to the world, but to me and my siblings he was the best. In life he worked hard to provide for us, and he taught us that hard work was its own reward. He took time to play with us. Whether it was on our backyard ball field or the ice rink we made, he was there. When we messed up as each one of us did, he might have been disappointed in us but never to the point that his love for us didn't show even more. He has been gone now for 23 years, and there are not too many days that pass without thoughts of him. He loved Jesus, loved my mom, and loved us kids...that's what made him special. So, dads, it doesn't take lots of money to make memories with your children (we had very little), it doesn't take fancy trips, (we had few), it doesn't take hours of planning (spur of the moment fun is the best). Make a memory today, so that your children will know you are the best dad in the world! To them you are!

****

Father's Day Cards and Grief

My dad passed away 24 years ago, and yet sometimes it feels like only yesterday. The first Father's Day after his death came only one month later. I remember standing in the card isle trying to find a card for my father-in-law. Not even thinking that this might invoke emotions I didn't want to deal with in the card isle. (Isn't that just like grief? It catches you off guard and hits you right between the eyes.) There in the middle of the card isle, I lost it. The tears would not stop. Trying to read the cards became a task I could not do. With each tear that rolled down my face, the words on the cards became a personal story of the emotions I was trying to hide. The people on both sides of me were uncomfortable with my lack of control at trying to pick out a card. What do you do with an uncontrollable crying woman picking out a card? Yup....you're right. Nothing! Realizing I would not be able to complete this seemingly easy task, and sensing some distinct stares, I put the cards down and walked away. Today, I am reminded of that day when grief was overwhelming.... when my emotions were unlocked...and when I realized I would no longer celebrate a Father's Day again with my dad on earth. Knowing that he is in heaven makes it much easier, and time does heal some of the emotions. So today I will say Happy Father's Day dad...in heaven. I'm saving up lots of hugs for you... love you so much and missing you every day.

****

Father's Day

I have loved looking at all the Father's Day tributes. My dad passed away 25 years ago. He was a good man. Loved his family, provided for his family and loved the Lord. I came across this picture of him when he was probably 5 or 6 years old. It hit me today that the reason he grew up to be a good father was the way he was raised by his family. He was learning at a very young age how to work in a family with 11 siblings. He learned how to give and take, he learned that the world did not revolve around him...and he learned how to receive and give love. All you young parents out there that are raising your children...remember they will one day become someone's parents or husbands and wives. What you do right now will be a direct result in how they learn to parent, and how they learn about relationships. You are their teachers. My grandparents did well, and I get to say Happy Father's Day with a smile because they taught my dad what true love is.

Missing you everyday Dad, Happy Father's Day in Heaven...

****

Memories of Thanksgivings Past

Seriously, next week is Thanksgiving! Am I the only one that Thanksgiving Day creeps up on? Right along with those of you who post daily in November what you're thankful for, I too, am thankful. One of the many things I am thankful for are memories. It is because of them I am able to close my eyes and be transported back to a Thanksgiving Day of my youth. I can hear the sounds of preparation coming from the kitchen as my mom starts her task of cooking a turkey, while we are still in bed. Of course, there is coffee brewing; the smell permeates through the whole house. There is quiet conversation between my mom and dad, and I can hear the sound of the pages being turned as my dad is reading his morning paper. It's Thanksgiving at the Campbell house.

Looking back, I am sure my mom must have been preparing for this one day all week. I remember knowing I would get some banana bread, that was my favorite...with walnuts. Oh, my mom baked pies, dinner rolls, and made a tasty cranberry salad, but I am pretty sure it was us girls that peeled the potatoes to be mashed for the soon to be devoured meal. Our turkey was huge, and we all wanted to get the wish bone. Anyone excited about that this year? It seems like there was always a guest or two at our table; Thanksgiving Day was no different. Finally, it was time to eat. We would gather around the table, with much conversation, watching as all the food was being placed on the table, would there even be room for it all? Yummy! Before we could dig in, we knew it was time to give thanks. We didn't hold hands, but we all bowed our heads as my father would thank God for our blessings. We sure did not have much when it came to material things, but the best blessing then and still is today are those that we love around our table. Thank you, God, for memories that never grow old.

****

Lesson Learned

Thanksgiving in Nashville, Tennessee has become almost a tradition for Paul and me. Since my dad passed away 23 years ago, we have made the trip every year to spend the holiday with mom. Oh, we always have plenty to eat at our Thanksgiving feast and we usually have no trouble finding things to do, but this year I wanted to also observe how my mom was getting along. She just turned 90, is still very independent and she is not ready to say goodbye to the place she calls home, much to her kids' dismay. This year while watching mom, she taught me another valuable lesson. On Thanksgiving morning there was a knock on her door and a 10-year girl was there wanting to see her. She lives just a few houses down from mom. I watched as my mom scooped this girl up in her arms with a big hug, and I noticed that this girl did not budge from my mom's embrace. Mom introduced us and she shared that this was the little girl she takes to church with her each week. I thought that was pretty cool... (how many of us do that?) After some small talk, the girl told me that she had not been doing very well in school. It didn't take me long to realize why. Her mom had died, so she went to live with grandma. She then experienced her grandmother dying too and is now living with an aunt. My mom started to encourage her to do better in school, to work hard and bring her grades up. Her incentive: If she brought her grades up my mom would take her out to a restaurant to eat. On Thanksgiving Day, she told my mom that she has done just that. From failing to excelling...she was excited to tell mom, and to find out when they would go out to eat. The lesson I learned was that no matter how old you are, as long as you have breath there is always someone who you can help. I need to be more aware of those that God is placing in my path. How about you? Oh, FYI...I think my mom is doing fine...but I would still like her to come to Michigan.

****

Thanksgiving

I will check in like many others today and say Happy Thanksgiving. I am sincerely thankful. Even though right now I am enjoying a morning coffee in a warm home, I know that many are cold and have no shelter. Today I will have a feast of turkey and pies with family and yet many I know are having a hard time even getting up to face another day, let alone a day where everyone is celebrating. They have lost loved ones or jobs, have crumbling marriages, or are dealing with stressful custody issues. So, in your joy today, be sensitive to the pain others are experiencing. They will be sitting next to you; they may have a smile on the outside but inside they will be dying. So, hang in there, my friends; today I am thankful for each of you.

****

This Too Will Pass

My mom was good at repeating teaching sentences. You know those sayings that sometimes you want to forget but are ever ingrained in your memory. I often hear her voice in my head: "Treat others as you would want them to treat you." "You make your bed...you lay in it." (my all-time favorite...NOT). "Don't go to bed angry" the list could go on and on.... But this morning I heard her loud and clear as I was feeling sorry for myself with an ankle that just doesn't want to heal as fast as I would it like to. I thought I ordered the "Hot and Now" recovery plan, but I find I am on the "Not Now,

42

or maybe not ever" plan. And her voice rings in my head... "This too shall pass," and I know it will. I hobbled out to get my hot drink fix this morning and turned on the faucet and nothing came out. Oh, where, oh where is my water? The sound of my mom's voice comes to me again: "This too shall pass." Just so you know, I also remember her encouraging us to figure things out, be creative, think outside the box! So, I will have you know that mom should be pretty proud of me this morning as I limped from faucet to faucet filling my coffee cup with the small stream of water that was still in the pipes. Yes, I enjoyed my coffee this morning, but I won't be having a second cup till after the well man comes!!! I hope you will all join me in this crazy time of life, saying...this too will pass.

****

The Gifts

I know it was Thanksgiving weekend, but I was blessed by receiving two Christmas gifts. One from my dad who passed away almost 23 years ago and one from my mother who is now 88 years old. These gifts were not something I could hold in my hands, but they will remain in my heart forever. The first gift was given through a young man named Matt K. Matt works at Gibson Guitar which is the same place my dad worked as an engineer designing guitars. He has not worked there in almost 30 years. You can imagine my surprise to find out that Matt tracked me down through my dad's obituary and Facebook. He has been researching some guitar designs that had my dad's initials and was impressed with the precision of his drawings and the excellent quality of his work, some of which are still being used. After hearing stories about my dad from the old timers at Gibson's, his curiosity got the best of him and he wanted to know more about Dale Leonard Campbell. Meeting him on Saturday in Nashville was a gift. Hearing stories about my dad and how others still remember his sense of humor and quality of workmanship 30 years later, well, it made my heart full. I am reminded of the verse in the Bible that speaks of the value of a good name. Thank you, Dad, for living out that verse. Proverbs 22:1.

Next post: the gift from my mom.

****

Gift number 2

As we were talking to Matt at a McDonald's in Nashville, we were very aware of a homeless woman sitting in the seat behind us. Her clothes were in disarray, her hair unkempt and she was sleeping. It wasn't too long before an employee came over and told the woman she was not allowed to sleep in the restaurant. We continued to talk and we did not notice the woman as she started to leave. I should say I didn't notice her leaving. My mom did. I saw my mom reach for her purse and with some money in her hand she rose to meet the woman. In the next moment I turned to see my mom embrace this woman as if she were her long lost friend, sitting down with her and listening to her story. Compassion overflowed from her heart. In the Bible it talks about Jesus seeing the hurting having compassion on them. I usually have compassion in my mind first, then I can talk myself out of helping. The gift from my mom was for me to see the need to move my compassion from my head to my heart where it can be overflowing like hers with the love of Christ. The picture she left in my mind I will never forget.

****

The Multiple Hats of Mom

My mom will be 91 years old soon, and I have been thinking about some episodes that she played the starring role in from my childhood. She has worn many hats as most moms do, but in my growing up years, every once in a while, she would be known as the chicken slayer. Yes, we had chickens roaming our yard. Not for pets, for food. When it was close to the weekend, my mom would don her hat that designated her chief chicken killer. She would scramble to find a chicken she could catch. That was no easy feat. But once she nabbed one, the chicken's fate was set. Grabbing an axe in one hand and holding that chicken head down with the other hand, she made one fell swoop of the axe to complete her job. The chicken's head was no longer attached to its body, but the body did not realize it yet. It continued to move around the yard without its head, and with me watching in awe (or maybe it was terror). What I do know is none of us kids ever messed with mom on the day she slayed the chickens. But we all loved the chicken dinners on Sundays at our house. As I sat and ate my chicken leg, I am sure my mind floated back to the day when the chicken I was putting in mouth had the bad luck of meeting up with the chicken slayer in my family. Thanks, Mom, for the memory.

****

The Final Move and a Treasure Found

I am well aware of how much Thanksgiving has changed this year. For the past 25 years Paul and I made our way to Nashville Tennessee to share the holiday with my mom. After my dad passed away, we felt like we needed to be with her on this holiday. Over the years we had many members of our family join us, and the path from Delton to Nashville was something we looked forward to and enjoyed. This year mom is here in Delton and our journeys to Nashville on Thanksgiving have ceased. My siblings and I moved her just last week to her home here in Delton. We packed and loaded and cleaned, shed some tears and shared laughter as we watched this chapter of her life, as well as ours close. In a pile of stuff that was to be put outside for pick up, I found it. This is an item that was in most homes in the 60's. How many times did I see my mom and dad around the table with this as a centerpiece? How many times did family and friends join them as they shared laughter as this piece of sleek beauty worked its magic? Too many to count, for sure. There it lay on the pile to be tossed. It was screaming at me to rescue it and take it home. I did, and this morning after a good cleaning, after the familiar sound of perking, I am enjoying a cup of coffee and remembering the smells and sounds this old coffee pot has built up for me in my life. Thanksgiving will be different this year, but some things never change family, coffee, friends...and the love of Jesus. Have a Happy Thanksgiving; and remember, there's always something to be thankful for...even a coffee pot from the 60's in the throw away pile.

****

A Fourth Grade Memory

Yesterday was the anniversary of the assassination of John F Kennedy. There was a spot on the news last night that reminded us just how it happened, who did it, and the turmoil it caused our country. I can vividly remember sitting in my fourth grade classroom, with Mrs. Jacoby as my teacher, when our class was interrupted by someone from the office, who whispered something in her ear, then she left. I am not sure if our teacher was crying, but I do remember her telling us, in a voice that we knew was serious, yet so sad, that the President had been shot. I think that was the first time I realized that evil existed. Why would someone do that? He had a wife and little kids. Fifty six years have passed and our country has had many moments that have been burned into our mind since then. Each one of us has had those times where we knew exactly what we were doing when tragedy struck. And yet, on that day 56 years ago, my teacher had us bow our heads and pray for our President and our country. On that day she taught me a great truth. When we don't understand what is happening all around us, just bow your head and pray.

****

2020 Why?

Along with many of you, as I sit back and observe what is going on in the world, I struggle with how to make sense of any of it. I am finding it hard to recognize even a small piece of the world I knew a few short months ago. Then a song floats into my mind. I remember the first time I heard the song; it was shared by a brave young woman, my friend's granddaughter, who was facing cancer again, and was losing her battle with it. She shared the song by Lauren Daigle, "I Will Trust In You." The song lyrics are about facing mountains that you don't know why you have to climb and asking the "why" questions and getting no response. As the song continues...the words come..."I will trust in You." I remember tears streaming down my face as I listened to this the first time. Trying to put myself in this young woman's shoes. She climbed the mountain of cancer, knowing her trust was in Jesus, and that someday He would make His plan clear to her. She sees clearly now the "why," and someday we will understand it too. So, today I struggle with the "why" questions of covid, and the "why" questions of politics, and the "why" questions of suffering. I must stop and remember that when the "why's" are not answered, my response has to be the words of that song...I will trust in You. Thank you, Jesus, for the memory of a song, the memory of Marissa, and the reminder that you are still in control.

****

December 2020

I just can't do it. Every year I tell myself this is the year that I get the modern Christmas tree look. You know, buying all the ornaments to match, the perfect swag of ribbon, and the tiny white lights that accent all the beautiful and perfect branches, which of course would be adorned with the most stylish and modern colors of the year. But it is not to be. My tree will never be a contender for the "Better Homes and Gardens" tree of the year; heck, it won't make it in the running for "Best of Show" in Barry County. Each year when I unpack the ornaments of Christmas past, it is like a trip back to a much simpler time. I have ornaments from my boys' first Christmas. Yes, they look marred by age, but their memory brings out a beauty that sees right past the wear and tear. Many ornaments were gifts from friends and families, and they bring a smile by just looking at them. A few picture ornaments find their way on my tree too, from grandchildren to deceased loved ones. They remind me that life is short and I must make the moments count. I also have tinsel on my tree. I know, I know...no one puts tinsel on their tree anymore. Well, I do. It is a reminder to me of days gone by when hanging tinsel was something to be taken very seriously. You had to place it on the tree, one strand at a time so it would nicely hang from the tip of the branches. It was also reused from year to year. If you were caught trying to glob them on, your privilege would be taken away. I learned to be careful with the tinsel and it is a good reminder to treat everything in life as carefully as I did the tinsel. I even thought about stringing some popcorn and cranberries this year to top off my eclectic tree, but for now, I must say to my modern tree urge that maybe next year will be the time to brush away the old and bring in the new. But I am pretty sure that won't happen, because I am seriously enjoying my colored lights, tinsel, and old ornaments. Hope you enjoy yours too.

****

Christmas Cookies and Grandkids

I am not sure how many Christmas cookie decorating times we have had with our grandkids. Since Abby is 18, I am going to guess at least seventeen. Seventeen years of flour all over the kitchen, kids sneaking a bit of dough with every cookie they cut out and of course...the licking of the frosting from their fingers as they intricately decorate each of their masterpieces. Okay, we do not get caught up in the germs we are passing around; what we do get caught up in is laughter and more laughter, and this year was not any different. Well, except they are older now, the highchairs have long been put away, and there is no need for much help. Most of them are teenagers, and even though they still sneak some raw dough and check out the frosting every now and then, it is something we all look forward to. Each year I am thankful that they still take time to come to Grandpa and Grandma's for some memories in the making, right along with some pretty yummy cookies! Taylor...we miss you! Abby, Lincoln, Micah, Seth, Adrian and Owen, thanks for making our day.

****

Christmas Cookies and Grandkids 2020

Some of you will say I am selfish. (I didn't socially distance.) I get it. But this morning I got Grandma hugs from all 6 of my grandkids that reported for Christmas cookie duty. It is getting more difficult to get them all together the older they become, but today was Christmas baking at Grandpa and Grandma's. They arrived at 9:00 am. Abby and Lincoln had jobs to go to in the afternoon, so we started early. For three hours, my house was filled with laughter and even some singing. Joining the laughter was some serious cookie baking and decorating. There was flour everywhere as the cookies were cut. The oven which was manned by grandpa turned out dozens of cookies that would soon have a coat of frosting and the individual design from each of my grandkids. Yes, they ate raw dough (I like that better than the finished cookie) Yes, they probably had frosting on their fingers that found a way into their mouths...and yes, I can say that even though 2020 has been a year to remember, so was our cookie baking day! Merry Christmas to you and yours...anyone want a cookie?

****

Memories, a Picture and Family

It's funny how a picture can transport you back to a memory you thought you had lost. So was the case this morning. The picture was posted on Facebook by a friend from school. It was a picture of her and her sister opening gifts of dolls in front of a tinsel-covered Christmas tree many years before. (Thanks Lou Ann Dehn Mitchell.)

As soon as I saw the photo, my mind shot back to a time at my house where I hugged a new doll. Her new-doll smell permeated my senses, and I was in love. A plain simple doll, not from a designer collection, not one that had to sit on a shelf, but one that I could claim as mine. In a family of 6, this was pretty important. She was mine, and I would take care of her. The memory of that day is etched in my mind forever. Many other memories floated to the forefront as I looked at that picture. I remember the way we hung our stockings on Christmas Eve. Now this was not what you might think; there were no pretty red fuzzy stockings, no embroidered name on the top to determine whose stocking was whose. Nope, ours were my dad's everyday socks. They were the biggest ones in the house. We placed our name on a piece of paper and tucked them inside so Santa would know whose stocking he was filling. Our stockings were hung, not by the chimney with care, they were hung on the wall...nothing special there. Our stockings were filled with some candy and fruit; a popcorn ball added to the loot. Christmas was simple in every way...the excitement it held for us kids is hard to describe today. I wonder though how many kids today start bounding down the stairs at 3:00am to see if Santa has been there? Six sets of feet every half an hour made a trek down those stairs to see if we could open gifts. For us there was no sleep on Christmas Eve, and I am pretty sure there was none for my parents either. Our gifts were open way before others in our town even got out of bed, and in the quiet of Christmas morning, in the little town of Prairieville...six little kids experienced again the wonder of giving, the joy of family and hope of a better tomorrow. I hope your Christmas Eve and Christmas brings you each of these things too.

****

The First Earth Day

I know that we are all in this together. Stay home, stay healthy has become our newest goodbye phrase. Going to any store makes you an active contestant of the game show we are now calling "Dodge the People." The newest accessory of the day has become the face mask, and life as we know it is slipping into history. Fifty years ago, today my sister Pat and I skipped school. Well, our mom knew about it, so maybe it wasn't skipping. It was Earth Day. The first one. And we missed it...on purpose. We just didn't think it was that important. Instead, we walked to school, just to check out what was going on without being a part of it. We didn't have to walk the whole three miles to school, because our Superintendent, (yes, the same one that we had visited before), picked us up and drove us the rest of the way. So, we looked in on the kids in school from the outside. We could see all the stuff they were doing but didn't have to partake. The next day, we went back to school. All was the same. Today, I feel like I am peering into a world gone crazy. I don't want to participate; I am watching from the outside. I am praying that tomorrow, or should I say May 1st, I can rejoin the world and go back to normal, whatever that might be. Happy Earth Day...who knew the event would last 50 years? Let's hope social distancing doesn't.

****

How to Plan for a New Kitchen

This morning I let myself be drawn again into one of those Facebook advertisements, and I ask myself "why?" Why do I even care about the 40 things you should never have in your kitchen? And yet, it draws me in. I tell myself I might get some ideas if I ever decide to redo the kitchen I have. Mind you, it's only 27 years old. But really how many of us remodel our kitchens annually? Well, anyway...I clicked on the site and what I discovered is that I really didn't need to waste my time. But it was worth a few laughs. Seriously, who puts those sites together? Let me see...never have white appliances, they tend to fade over time (well, mine still look white 27 years later). And for goodness sake wood cupboards are so out. (Guess what I have?) But painted ones are in...as long as they are not white because that is just too much white. Linoleum? A definite no-no. Short back splashes are not good, but tall ones are okay as long as they are not brick, and who would even dream to get spotted granite? Do any of you have a microwave? Those should be thrown out, and if you can't bring yourself to toss it, for gosh sakes do not have one of those above your cooking stove. Oops! Guess who has one there? No drapes allowed in the kitchen (I passed that one). No words on the walls.   Really? I kind of like mine. All in all, I guess I did learn that at my age, I could care less about what is going to pass as styling. I don't plan on moving out too soon, and I am not trying to impress anyone anymore...but when new owners take over my home someday, I wish I could see their response to my writing on the wall: "Many have eaten here, few have died!" Enjoy your kitchens.

****

Garage Sales and Covid June 2020

It's Friday, it's June, and finally my sister and I are going to try to find a few garage sales. This virus stuff has canceled so many things, but when it started to affect my garage sale Fridays, it was almost enough to put me over the edge. But today you might see us in the area as we look for the signs that say, "Garage Sale." We will be in the car that brakes for all signs alongside the road, we will be laughing when we realize it's a "house for sale," sign instead of a garage sale sign. We will be driving unknown roads looking for the best deal of the day as we try to bring a bit of normal to a world that is everything but. So, if you happen to run into us on our quest for hidden treasures today, know that our little corner of the world is being filled with smiles and laughter...wishing you the same.

****

Missing My Dad

April 11th....today is my niece's birthday...Happy Birthday Jennifer, and yesterday on April 10th was another niece's birthday, Denyel. April 13 is my granddaughter Taylor's birthday, and I am pretty sure about this time you are saying why did I need to share this family history with you?

A good question. But you see sandwiched in between those days is April 12th. No birthdays on that day in our family, but it is a date that I will never forget. It is the day my dad changed his address from earth to heaven. I have pondered the timing of his death, right smack dab between family celebrations. I know he had nothing to do with the time he died, but I do think God was gracious to us as He took my dad home in the midst of family joy. I will choose to continue to see joy and happiness as long as I am here, because during a week of celebration my dad got to have the best celebration of all. Oh, it does not take away from the longing I have to hear his laughter again, or to have him give me a hug one more time or just to listen to him sing, but it does make me smile knowing that he is with the King!!! Missing you everyday dad! I can't wait to see you again.

****

The Cry of the Voiceless

I have always been Pro-Life. You could say it is one of my passions. I have seen the damage that has lasted for years in the lives of women who have made the choice to abort. My heart has broken for the grief experienced in their lives. I have cried with women who 30 years ago heard and believed the lie that their problem could be over in a few minutes, when in reality they live with heartache and pain every day. Today I watched the movie "Unplanned" and was reminded why we must not give up being a voice for the voiceless. An evil has crept into our society while most of us were sleeping! For those who have made this choice, there is healing and hope; for those about to make this decision, know that it will be a day that will be burned in your mind forever, a decision you can't undo. For the rest of us, pray, be willing to help, and show love and compassion. We must never stop fighting for them.

****

March for Life

Fridays are my days to run around and play catch up from the week. So, I just sat down and decided to check Facebook. Scrolling down the posts I noticed someone had posted a feed from The March for Life Rally in Washington today, and I watched. And I read posts. And I was sad in spirit. I don't ask any of you to agree with me, but I truly can't get my mind around the fact since 1973 we have lost 60 million children to abortion. 60 Million! Each of us knows someone who has had an abortion, who thought that was the only choice they had. I have walked alongside those who have regretted their choice, some who choose to bury it deep and try to forget, and some who have carried the scars for years. I too, had been faced with that choice many years ago, and I did choose Life. It makes me no better than the one who didn't. But the sadness is still in my soul for the lives lost before they have had a chance to live! I hope one day that even if abortion remains legal, there would be no one wanting to have one. That LIFE is what we would all choose. I hope your heart hurts too from this unnecessary loss.

****

We Are The World

Crying children ripped from their parent's arms is something that no one wants to see. Yet here we are looking at it on every news outlet in America. We are being told how heartless we are as a country. I read a response to a post that said, "How can any of us even sleep at night and call ourselves 'Americans' with this going on?" I hear the emotional outcry ....and yet most of us have slept very well over the past 40 plus years as we have allowed and defended the right to rip our own children from our wombs. Their cries are silent to us, but they are still crying. We watch daily as people in this country who have committed crimes are being removed from their crying children. Not easy for those kids either. I really don't have an answer to our border problems.

This world has many things wrong with it, but as the old saying goes...WE ARE THE WORLD! Does my heartbreak for the families? Yes....does my heartbreak for those who have never been given the chance to breathe? Yes...Does my heartbreak for all those who are pulled away from family...Yes...Lord help us find our way.... we are so lost!

****

Where were you?

Do you know what you were doing 45 years ago today? Yeah, me neither. But 45 years ago, today, our world changed. Some were glad, some were shocked, most like me had no clue what had been legalized. I was busy trying to raise a baby born a few months earlier when I was 17. I am sure I gave little thought to the law that had just been passed that gave women the right to abort the baby in her womb. Yet, that decision is the reason I am the Director at The Delton Women's Center. I have seen much sadness, many tears and many unanswered questions, from women of all ages who thought that abortion was their only option. It's the questions they have that haunt their sleep at night. You know the questions. The what if's: What if I had chosen life, and then that question leads to more, what would my child look like? What would they be doing? Would they have children? The list goes on and on. To me this issue is not political. You can pass laws that make things legal, but it never makes them right. I know many of you will not agree with me; I don't expect you to. I speak from a heart that is tired of hearing stories of unimaginable sorrow and pain, where too many lives have been wounded from a war waged in the depth of their souls. It is time to stop. Choosing Life has always been a part of God's plan.

****

Memorial Day

As a young girl growing up in the big town of Prairieville, this was the day that put our town on the map. As a kid I am not sure I understood just what all the excitement was about. What I did know is that there was more coffee made at our house than usual that morning and there would be lots of people stopping in to visit. The cemetery was mowed neat as could be, and there would be flowers on most gravesites. Flowers left not so much for those who had passed, but for the living to remember those who had passed. From the time our feet hit the floor the morning of Memorial Day we were on the move. Walking up and down the one street in Prairieville, we watched as people lined up their cars alongside the road in anticipation of the parade. My sister Pat and I would stop and chat with some, wave at others, and feel the excitement of the coming parade. Then we would hear it...a siren. The parade was about to start. As we watched the soldiers pass by, I still don't think I realized the parade was about them. Fast forward 50 plus years, and tomorrow you will still find me at the Memorial Day parade in Prairieville, I will walk down the street and chat with old friends, and wave at others. Some things just don't change much, but tomorrow when the sirens sound, and I see the soldiers, I know all too well this parade is for them. As they pass by, some people might be talking, some might be clapping. For some like me you might see a tear. Because somewhere between youth and adulthood life happens, and you know that those men and women deserve our utmost respect and honor not just on Memorial Day but every day! Thank you to my dad, my father-in-law, my brothers, and my nephew for your service. Tomorrow is Memorial Day... stop and remember.

****

Memorial Day 2019

I stayed so busy today that I am just sitting down to process this very important day, and I am realizing its importance more with each passing year. I have been at the parade in Prairieville as long as I can remember. There were the times I marched it in as a Bluebird girl, and then as a band member and even a few times as a Den mother, but mostly I have watched. It really doesn't change much. Veterans first, followed by fire trucks, a marching band, Scouts, and of course, a few miscellaneous tractors thrown in the mix. A perfect parade in small-town America. This parade was replayed over and over in small towns across our nation today. There really isn't anything unique about our parade. We all know it's not the parade that makes it special, it is the participants. The ones we watch...because we know them. The veterans in our parade live among us. We know the band members, the fire truck drivers and the scouts. So, we watch. As the service in the cemetery started, the veterans stood at attention until it was their turn to shoot the guns. I braced myself for the loud sound that would come, (they always make me jump) and as the Taps were played, my eyes fell on my brother. He stood at attention....and I wondered where his mind might be trailing off to. Was he reliving his time in Vietnam? Was he thinking about friends that never came home? Was he wondering why he had been so severely wounded?

I will never know, but for that moment in my heart, I understood why we must never forget. And why we call it Memorial Day. To all our soldiers, veterans, and those who gave their lives for us.... You are Heroes.

****

May 2020 Memorial Weekend

Okay, I went to our cottage on Memorial Day Weekend, and yes, I must admit my family joined me. Most times we stayed under or at least right on the mark of the 10 people limit, (oops just recounted...we were over 10) and sometimes we had a few more...all in all it was a great weekend. The weather was perfect, the food was yummy, and laughter echoed in all we did. I realized later we never turned on the TV, hardly checked social media...and my level of frustration went down. Since there are so many things I like on

Facebook, but also many things I don't like, I decided today that any political ad, no matter who posts it will be deleted from my feed as soon as I see it. I will choose when and who I will vote for, whether it is standing in line or by mail. I will decide what I let my eyes look on and with what I fill my mind. I am done with conspiracy theories, who did or didn't do something soon enough, when and why you wear a mask...I will look forward to those of you who post family things, pictures of smiles, and those who challenge me with educational posts...just letting you know my new normal...not doing the political stuff anymore. Maybe it's time you join me. I can't believe how easy it is!!!!

∗∗∗∗∗∗∗∗∗∗∗

Pride of Family

This morning I am finding myself still reeling from the joy I received as I watched my brother Bruce get inducted into Delton High School Sports Hall of Fame last evening. Dustin M. and David O. along with Bruce have earned their place in the Hall of Fame at Delton. But it was seeing my brother as he stood in the middle of the gym floor, a little bit aged, a little nervous, along with some well-deserved pride that got to me. While we all listened as the announcer read his accomplishments, it wasn't surprising that the applause from the crowd came at many times during the announcing. It was when the announcing moved to his time in Vietnam, his leadership in the Marines as a young 19-year-old, his being wounded in combat, and receiving many military awards that the crowd could not remain seated. They stood and applauded and applauded some more. It was then that I saw my brother start to shed a tear, along with many of us in the crowd. He is a true hero. His accomplishments on the field were good, his military experience changed his life, but it is what he has managed to do after all he has been through that has touched so many lives. He gave of himself to our country, to our community, to many kids over the years that called him coach, and to his family. So, thank you Delton Schools for the honor you gave to my brother; you allowed others to see my brother how his family has always seen him.

∗∗∗∗∗∗∗∗∗∗∗

Remember 9-11

I wish we could go back to the time when 9-11 was a date I remembered because it is my niece's birthday. A time when an attack on the United States was almost unthinkable, a time when terrorism was thought of as happening "over there somewhere" ...surely not here. But then 18 years ago Sept 11th brought a whole new meaning to that date. And our country wept, and we mourned. For those of us who witnessed this devastation, we will carry in our hearts the tragedy of that day forever. Never being able to remove from our minds what our eyes watched as the terror unfolded. How could we? The horror of watching firefighters bravely enter a building of no escape, and yet, they entered. The unbelievable sounds of people hitting the ground as they plummeted out of the towers, the look of shock and sadness on people as the streets of New York were covered with the dust of the twin towers. We watched the innocence of our country leave, never to return. The Pentagon, Flight 93, The Twin Towers are seared in our minds like it happened yesterday. So today, I will also remember that day 18 years ago, and along with that I will remember the glimpses of love we witnessed on that day and the days that would follow. Airplanes might have destroyed our buildings, and taken many loved ones, but they did not destroy America...and now when we hear "Let's Roll" it should remind us to be as determined as The Flight 93 passengers... Never give up!

****

Spring of 2020—Covid Crazy

Is seeing really believing? I am sad to see so many posts of hatred toward one another. As a recently appointed couch sitter and Facebook scroller with friends who have differing opinions on everything, it is hard to get a handle on what is true. I wasn't at the rally in Lansing, but I have seen reports of ambulances being blocked and reports that a hospital was not accessible, and then I saw reports that said just the opposite. Who do you believe? I see posts that say the virus numbers are being skewed, I see posts that say to get ready, because the virus is coming for all of us. I see posts telling us to stay home but support our local restaurants with take-out. I see a lot of people trying to make sense of a world gone crazy...and we are fighting against each other. I am not sure the rally in Lansing did anything either way, but I do know I am thankful to live in a country where we as citizens are still allowed to voice our opinions, whether I agree with them or not. I am thankful that I have friends who don't always see eye to eye with me. I might not agree with them, but I respect them enough to try to understand the reasons they feel a certain way. I see a country that wants to get back to work, to not spread this virus, and one that is trying to figure it out...I have hope that we will get there, I just hope we don't destroy ourselves in the process.

****

April 2020

Reality check COVID-19

I am not motivated. I can't begin to tell you how many areas in my home that I should be organizing, and decluttering. Last week, the week before that and the week before that are all a blur in my mind. They have not resulted in any major projects being done; they have not even seen baby steps to getting anything accomplished. Yes, Covid 19...you have shown me who I am. And to be honest with you...I am not that crazy about the real me in the last few weeks. Those of us who love being around people, who get energized by the interaction of meeting new people, checking in on others, visiting friends...well...this stay-at-home policy has become our worst nightmare. I never realized that by taking away a part of who I am, (yes, I am a people person) could have such a dramatic impact on the other areas in my life. Nothing seems to be lining up. So, yesterday I went against the governor's orders, and met a friend for a face-to-face distanced meeting. I can't begin to tell you how good it was to listen, talk and share our lives with each other even if it was only for an hour or so. Did our meeting give me energy to come home and tackle things that need to be done? Heck no... But it reminded me again of what is more important in this world, and it is not organizing and decluttering; it is people. I might not be happy in the person I have been over the past few weeks, but I am ever so thankful that God placed a love for others in my being, and that I am not the best I can be without all of you. COVID-19, it's time to GO!

****

A Time for Laughter

I never know what will trigger a writing attack, but this morning it was watching an ad for "Laugh Fest" in Grand Rapids. A weekend of laughs, that sounds right up my alley.

I learned to laugh from the best. Every person in my family growing up taught me that pulling jokes on each other, well, is just what you do. A daily family joke would be to make the phone ring into our home, answer it, then call to a family member and tell them they had a phone call, only to find no one there. Or we might painstakingly fill an empty dish detergent container with string, and when our target came into sight, we would squirt out the string...they would think it was dish soap.

Of course, with all the laughter at our home, we knew we had to share the fun. So, my sister Pat and I took our laugh show on the road...to school! The string detergent got a few laughs, but it wasn't the trick of the century we were looking for. So, we set out to find just the right way to get some laughs. A little imagination here and a few ingredients there, before too long we were looking at our masterpiece. Drum Roll please... We were sure this would place us in the best trick of the year category...and seriously it might have, except for that little part we didn't plan on...a trip to the Superintendent's office.

Yes, we were looking at our chocolate-covered cotton balls. They were a beautiful sight before our eyes. For sure, this was going to be a good day at school. The excitement we had on the bus that morning I am sure showed in the big smiles on our faces. Entering the school, we began to share our chocolates with anyone that wanted them. And they all wanted them. Oh, the joy of sharing...It wasn't too long before we heard a little gagging, and then it happened. The chocolate balls that had gone into their mouths so easy came out with a spewing sound that echoes in my ears today. And we laughed, all the way to the Superintendent's office. There he was Basil Johnson. He had a presence about him that screamed, "Don't mess with me!" Two little girls stood before him; their fate rested in the words that were to come out of his mouth. In the wisdom of Solomon, (I wonder if he was chuckling under his breath) he looked at us, and said, "You need to go and pick up every cotton ball that was spit out." We breathed a sigh of relief and dutifully obeyed. I am sure as we picked up the left-over cotton balls in the hallway, our minds were already thinking of the next thing we could do that would bring us some laughs. There are a few that are coming to mind, but I will save them for another day. Thankfully for us, it was the early 60's, because in today's world I am sure there would have been an arrest, a trip to juvie, and probation to follow. Yikes...

****

Summer 2020

I can tell you that this social distancing is a hard one for me to get a handle on. If you are usually a hugger at heart, well, this just goes against who you are. But I am managing to stay away and to keep my hands to myself so you can all breathe a sigh of relief. I promise if I see you, I will say "hi" from a distance.

But laughter...that is something I can't live without, so I hope this story helps you connect with the lighter side of life, since we certainly all can use a laugh nowadays.

I like to think of our family when I was growing up as a cross between the Walton's, Little House on the Prairie and The Little Rascals. There wasn't much that we kids as a group didn't think of getting into. We were always on the lookout for the next way to trick someone, as I've said before. We took our tricks on the road often...to school. There we had a captive audience. I am not sure if the school office had our family name circled in big letters on a chalkboard somewhere, but I have to think they were very familiar with it. Especially after the day some invisible ink and my teacher met up close.

As I recall, it was a history class, and from my memory the teacher was one that didn't laugh much. I thought it was my job to help her find her sense of humor. (In hindsight, not a good idea.) As she stood teaching in front of the class, her white blouse taunting me from my chair, I thought "This is the time!" I made a move toward her with my invisible ink bottle in hand, and passing by her, I squirted a stream of dark ink on her beautiful white blouse. I had let the class in on my soon-to-be trick, and the class laughed (which is what I wanted anyway), but for some reason that is not the response I got from the teacher. I remember words streaming from her mouth: "You are going to buy me a new blouse!" and "Why did you do that?!'" It was at that moment I realized that if the ink didn't disappear, I was going to be in trouble. Well, I was going to be in trouble anyway. Thankfully, about the time the teacher was getting ready to have me sent to the office, the ink started to disappear. Yes, the stunt worked. I was in the clear. Well, almost. I am pretty sure I found myself again standing in front of the Superintendent pleading my case. Fast forward a few years...as an adult I attended a church and guess who was playing organ at the church? You guessed it; my teacher from sixth grade. I never mentioned the ink scene, and neither did she. I guess some things are better left in the past. Like invisible ink and teachers.

****

Happy Birthday, James.

I am excited to share with all of you today that my baby is 540 months old. Yes, I know it is hard to believe... but it is true. There are so many things he is able to do now. Those few steps that he took at 8 months, well, you will be happy to know he has mastered walking and moved onto running with no problem. He graduated from doing chores around the house, to a real paying job. Way to go, James! Under expert tutelage he learned the skills of food preparation, and you can find him at any given time cooking up a storm in his kitchen for his two sons. He can drive, he can cook, he does laundry and best of all, he can still make me laugh. I just wish when he was over last Sunday that I had taken a picture of him laying on a blanket with a sign that said, "Today I'm 540 months old." Next year for sure. Happy Birthday, James Matthew. God smiled at me when he placed you in our family.

****

August 2019

It was nice getting away for a few days. Now that we are home, I have had a little time to mull over a few experiences that I am sure will turn into great memories for future reference soon. For all of you that do get-a-ways without a hitch, they must be really boring, because all our memorable times come from the unplanned; at least that is the story I am going to stick with. Twice on our trip that great piece of invention called a GPS had us in places that we didn't want to be.

Okay, the first time was my fault. When I punched in Moundsville, I just figured it would take me to the city.... wrong! After a few hours of driving and wondering why we were not going in the direction I thought we should go, I realized that there is a Moundsville Street, in a city toward the bottom of Ohio. Fine and dandy if you are heading that way; not so good if you wanted to be heading to the top part of West Virginia...and right then and there plan A became plan B. Who knew? Unplanned, but manageable.

Day two I was sure would be much better...but who am I trying to kid? Our GPS directed us to WV, and once there we punched in our first tourist destination. Forgetting all too soon our bout with the mountain last year in California, we listened to a voice in our car that said turn left, and we followed it. It was a county road and it was paved for about three miles. Three miles of smiles; the next ten, tears and fears.

Okay. Many of you are saying, why not turn back? That was my question too. Paul assured me that it would be okay; it's a county road. That was before the mud, falling rocks sign, the washed-out roads, the stones, the no way to turn around, and no way for two cars to pass each other in view. I seriously thought we would be met by a distant relative of the Hatfield's and McCoys with a rifle saying we were trespassing in their hollow! I am pretty sure the scenery was beautiful, the air was clean, but I was jumping for joy when I saw a beautiful paved road heading for a city! You just can't plan for stuff like this. We are so into the unplanned, (not really) ...but at this stage in life...when it happens, you just learn to roll with it!

****

Do You Know Your Neighbor?

Growing up in the 60's in small-town USA brings to mind things we did as routine that are nonexistent today. Making your own Valentines, picking flowers for May Day baskets and going Christmas caroling are a few. There were also times in our town when someone would pass away and I would go knocking on doors to ask if anyone would like to donate money either for flowers or just to give to the deceased families. At a young age, I became aware of the sadness of grief and loss but was also included in taking part in helping those who were hurting in my community. Memories of my mom and the neighbors preparing meals for the family who had lost loved ones are seared in my mind. You knew your neighbors and you knew when they hurt. Today I have been reminded of those special days due to the passing of my neighbors' father. I didn't know him, and I really don't know my neighbors that well either, but I will send a card with my deepest sympathy, as my heart will long for the simpler days of really knowing and caring about your neighbor. Maybe I should bake a cake and just take it across the street.... knowing being neighborly starts with me!

****

Garage Sales and Family

It's that time of year again. On Fridays you will find my sister, my mom and once in a while a grandkid set out to tackle the Garage and Estate Sale scene. Oh, we feel we are pretty much experts in this hobby. We can spot the ones that think they will make a killing on their stuff, (prices too high) we can tell those who want to just get rid of items (prices really cheap) and those that like to barter a bit...but then we wander into an Estate Sale. Whole house furnishings for sale. Sometimes it is overwhelming to roam from room to room and pick through a person's whole life. It is all right there. I find myself wondering what the people were like that owned all of these things. I can tell a little by the books they read what they were interested in. Birds, history, science, it's all there. I am often drawn to small items and as I pick up an angel with a broken wing, or a bird that lost its beak, or maybe a cup with a crack in it, I see nothing of value in them. So why did they keep these broken pieces? Why do I hang on to the things that I do? Well, they have a value to me. A gift given by someone special. A souvenir of a rock from a vacation, a dish with a crack in it that used to be my grandma's. No one looking at my things will understand why I have kept them either. So, I wonder when I am gone and someone is looking through my things what will they learn about me? All the material things we accumulate here on earth will be left for someone else to use or dispose of. What story will your things tell about you? Storing up our treasures in heaven is what we strive for. The things that can't be bought. But I can tell you while I am still here, I will continue to enjoy the search for the best garage sale deal of the day!!!!! I am pretty sure after I'm gone,

they will be saying, "I wonder what garage sale she got this from!"
Love my Fridays.

****

Christmas time

My husband says there is nothing like a death to cheer me up. He says it with a smile, because he knows I enjoy watching shows like 48 Hours, Dateline and Forensic Files. I am not sure why they intrigue me. It's been that way for as long as I remember. My heart is always saddened by the way we humans treat each other. We all scream, "Love our neighbors," but have a hard time loving our family. During the holidays the domestic violence incidents escalate. Ask any 911 operator or police officer and I think they would verify it. So, this year as we enter the season of Thanksgiving, Good Will, and Peace on Earth, let's try to really live it. Let's remember it's not in the gifts you give, it's not in the gifts you receive and it's not in the parties you attend. It's what's in your heart! Does your heart break for those hurting? Does your heart long for peace? Does your heart love? Because true love is what this world needs, and we can't do it on our own. It comes from the Baby in the manger. Look for Him this year and when you find Him, He will fill your heart with everything you need!

****

Moms, Birthdays and Sons

You know I have always wanted to do the mom thing like the mom in City Slickers. The mom calls her son, played by Billy Crystal every year at the exact moment of his birth, describes her labor pains, how long she labored, and basically her whole birth experience, then wishes him a Happy Birthday. It was funny then and it still makes me laugh now. Tomorrow is my son James' birthday. As moms, we stress over how to raise responsible kids. We want to raise kids that contribute to society, that treat others with kindness, and to make the world a better place. We do this job knowing full well that we mess up, we yell when we are supposed to speak softly, we get angry and go from 0-60 in two seconds, totally losing our cool, and yet we also stand over that same child while he sleeps and realize what a gift they are, and we tremble at the responsibility given to us. Then one day you turn around and you realize your job of being a hands-on mom is over. You look at your adult child and you can't believe that they have become exactly what you wanted them to be. It is then that you know full well you really didn't do this parenting thing alone. You know that God walked with you through every screw up, every harsh and angry word, and somehow brought about the miracle of a grown son who is everything you had ever hoped for. Wishing you a Happy Birthday, James Matthew, and one of these years, I am going to do the City Slicker mom thing... 😊

****

Do a Kind Act

Right now, people are gathering at the funeral home in Delton to celebrate the life of Veronica Cimala. She lived a very long time in the Delton area, and was well known by many. She had a laugh that you would recognize two isles over in the grocery store, and a voice that spoke with a very Polish accent. She was Mrs. Cimala to me, but to my mom she was so much more. When my family moved into Delton in 1955, mom was 26, had 6 children and my dad was going to school at the Vet school on Pine Lake...now MCTI. (Michigan Career and Technical Institute)

We moved into a big two story brick house on M43 and set out to do life in Delton. That's where Mrs. Cimala comes in. She was the first person to welcome my mom, she brought in food and even invited us to her house for meals. This by no means was an easy task since she had several children too. Her acts of kindness more than 60 years ago still have an impact on my mom today because she will never forget her or the kindness that she received from her. Not sure why I thought I should share this, except to let you know that those acts of kindness to others live on for years.

They sure have in our family. Mrs. Cimala lived her faith. I pray each of us will too.

****

Birthdays and Sons

Do you ever wonder as you look back on your life how you ever survived some of those difficult times? Well, today has been a day of reflection for me. Maybe it is because my youngest son James Matthew has a birthday tomorrow. For all you young moms out there who are pulling your hair out trying to raise your kids to become responsible adults, thinking to yourself that you are a failure...stop...breathe...look around you. God has given you the ability, the wisdom and strength to do this job. He does not expect perfection; He does not want super moms...what He does want is for you to lean on Him. It is no different for the mom who is 15 or 63. You see, this thing called motherhood does not end when the child reaches 18 years. It never ends. Oh, your children won't need you to clothe and feed them forever, but before long your role will change. It weaves in and out of friendship, counselor and confidant. But it never goes away. So, today as I reflect on the very young mom, I was 43 years ago, getting ready for my second son James to join our family, I am filled with a joy and love for Jesus that is almost unspeakable, for He never gave up on this mom, and He has allowed me watch my sons grow up and become godly men, in spite of my screw ups. So, James, your kindness, compassion and crazy sense of humor are only a few of the many things God has blessed you with, and I will always be grateful that He picked me to be your mom. You made it easy. Happy Birthday one day early.

****

Birthdays and Sons

How is it possible that my son is 45 years old today? Seriously, wasn't it just yesterday that he was riding up and down our driveway with his Hot Wheels bike, or making a mess as he ate popsicles in the summer sun? As a mom it's hard to admit those days are gone and now, they live only in the memories of the past. But that is life. So, to my son, Steven, I wish you a HAPPY BIRTHDAY and I pray you will have many more years of following the path God has planned for you. Today I realized that 45 years did pass in the blink of an eye.

****

Helping in time of Need

Hurricane Harvey. Its devastation is beyond comprehension for those of us who sit in our dry homes, having food in our cupboards and a warm place to sleep. My heart goes out to the people of Texas and what they will face in the coming months. It seems there is sadness everywhere. But today, I saw hope for our country. It was a few short weeks ago that the only thing plastered all over the news was racial strife and hatred. As much as I hate all that Hurricane Harvey has destroyed, there is one thing it has restored: my faith in humanity. Today, I saw people who owned boats lined up waiting for the chance to go and rescue someone trapped. They didn't line up in several lines, like this line only rescues Mexicans, this line, African Americans, this line only Christians. No. Only one line, to help anyone who needed it. They were willing to risk their lives for a brother or sister in need. Period. So, today as I pray for those in desperate need in Texas, I will also thank God for giving me a glimpse of humanity at its best.

****

Mother's Day

I remember as a little girl, my sister and I would make our mom breakfast in bed. We would probably burn the toast, make a mess pouring the orange juice, and there is no way we could have done eggs Sunny Side up.... they would turn out scrambled every time. Yet, as we approached her bedroom, our hearts were filled with the anticipation of the joy we would see in her eyes as we made our way through the door. And we saw it every time. She would act surprised, even though she had heard us in the kitchen for the last 30 minutes making a big mess. It was a simple act of giving to make her special day start out right. I'm sure we had a gift for her too, but you know the only thing I remember is seeing her eyes light up as we walked into her room. I am blessed to still have my mom. Time really doesn't change moms or kids much, because I still look for that glint of excitement in her eye. It doesn't come from breakfast in bed anymore, although if she were here, I would have loved to surprise her. So, Mom, on this Mother's Day I thank you for all you have done to make our home happy, for loving us and letting each of us think we were your favorite kid, and best of all thanks for still putting up with all six of us. I hope you have an amazing day......God blessed our family when He made you our MOM.

Life Lessons I Learned From the Pulpit

(Each year as I approach Holy Week, there is always something to write about, so I have several writings and thoughts on the days leading up to Easter…I hope you will enjoy them and learn from them too.)

Maundy Thursday

It's the Thursday before Easter, this evening we remember Jesus as he ate his last supper with His disciples. He was not only preparing himself for what was to come, He also knew one of his disciples would betray Him and yet He continued to teach His disciwples how to be a servant as He rose from the table and washed their feet. Humbling. To think the Son of God would stoop to wash their filthy feet. I'm sure it was almost more than they could imagine. Washing feet! When was the last time any of us stooped to wash someone's feet. And yet, Jesus still calls us to be servants. What does that look like today? Each one of us must search our hearts for our own area of service to others, for like Christ demonstrated we are not here to be served but to serve. How will you serve your Savior?

****

Judas, Jesus, Friend

My writing today was really for me, but maybe you can identify with it too...

How do you describe a friend? Faithful? Loyal? Kind? Considerate? Trusting? Those are a few of the things that come to my mind when I think of a friend. Since it is getting close to Easter, I like to scan the passages in the Bible leading up to the crucifixion. I certainly know the story. I am sure you do too. Today, I was reading from Matthew, the 26th chapter. I read about Jesus as He prayed in the garden, while his disciples slept, Jesus, as he was getting arrested. The garden scene is being played out. That is when I spotted it...Judas! We all know that he was the leader of the pack so to say, of those who would arrest Jesus. There he was coming right toward Jesus, and he called to Jesus, saying, "Rabbi," then kissed Him. What caused Judas to betray his teacher? He had walked with him three years, saw His miracles, learned from Him, and still betrayed Him. I just can't wrap my mind around that. But what comes next is something I will never be able to understand, but I am ever so grateful for. Jesus looked at Judas, with eyes of love, and called him

Friend! Friend? Really, friend? Judas, the jerk, the black sheep of the group, Judas, the shady treasurer. It's right there in verse 50: Jesus, calling him friend. My stomach at this point is churning because I know many times, I have failed Jesus. I can remember many times in my life that I have done things that have betrayed Christ. The sins I have committed against Him haunt my soul. Forgiven doesn't always mean forgotten on our part. But there it is. For me today and hopefully for you too, Jesus knows all my sins, He knows my heart and thankfully still looks at me and calls me, "Friend." Like the old hymn says, "What a friend we have in Jesus."

****

Good Friday

What I can't seem to get out of my mind today is that Jesus knew on Friday He would be dead. But today is Monday and what does He do? As far as I can tell, He did exactly what He had been doing for the past three years, teaching, inviting and loving people.

Fast forward 2,000 years. If I knew today on Monday that my final day on earth would be Friday...what would I be doing?

What would you be doing?

****

Well, it's Good Friday,

I have always wondered about the reason we call it Good Friday. It was the day where nothing good appeared to be happening. It was a day that started out with illegal trials, severe beatings, mocking and humiliation, friends that denied you, and ended with a death. Not any normal death, but a painful agonizing death by being nailed to a cross. As hard as I try, I can't see anything good about this Friday. I, like the rest of Jesus' followers would not be finding any good about today. But the week is not over. His story is not today; it is Friday, but Sunday's coming!!!!

****

Good Friday and Friends

I woke this morning with a heart of heaviness. Two good friends of mine have members in their family fighting for their life.

One who has a dearly loved sister who appears to be in the end stages of life and one whose granddaughter is fighting yet another bout with cancer. And I ask, "why?"

Why does life have to be so hard? It's just not fair. Oh, but soon I am remembering that today is Good Friday, a day where "not fair" should have been heard from every lip in Jerusalem. But instead, their lips shouted, "Crucify Him!" So not fair!!! What Christ endured on the cross and that He defeated death so that we might have life was so "not fair" for Jesus. But He did it for us. My heart is still heavy for my friends and their families. Suffering and death of a loved one will always hurt. But they know Jesus means this is not the end for them, and since death is the reality for all of us, I pray that each of you will take a moment today and see how His "not fair" can mean eternal life for you.

****

Saturday

Well as far as the disciples could tell Jesus was dead. Crucified by the very people who had shouted praise to Him a week earlier. Dead. They saw His disfigured body; they might have even helped take Him off the cross. What a horrible task that would have been. There was no doubt; He was dead. So, I wonder what they thought about on Saturday, the day after. He told them He would rise after three days, but today is Saturday and He is dead. Can you imagine what was going through their minds? Was He the real son of God? Did they waste the last three years following a mere man who is now…dead? I ask myself what would I have been doing on that Saturday? Would I doubt? Would I run? Would I resume my life where I had left off three years earlier? But in their heart, they had hope. Hope and faith that HE was who He said He was. We know today is Saturday and He is dead. Hold on to hope, keep your faith, remember His love, because tomorrow is Sunday…. Wait and see.

****

Palm Sunday

Palm Sunday brings to memory a little girl waving Palm branches as she marched around the inside of the church. Today I watched the same type of procession, palms waving, and people of all

72

ages smiling to a song of a triumphal entry that took place many years ago. The crowd many years ago exploded with excitement, they screamed with cheers, they laid their coats down for the King riding a donkey. I'm sure I would have been there. Joining in with praises, knowing this was our man of the hour. I can't help but wonder what was going through Jesus' mind. They saw today, He saw Friday. They screamed for joy, He would soon hear the screams of "Crucify Him!"; they laid down their coats, He would soon lay down His life. So, I ask myself, what crowd would I have been in? Sadly, my answer is both. But thankfully the week is not over.

****

Children's Sermon and Palm Sunday

I get to do children's sermon in our church on Sunday. It will be Palm Sunday. Of course, we will talk about parades, isn't that what Palm Sunday starts with? Jesus, entering the city of Jerusalem on a donkey while a crowd of people cheered for him. A parade of one! How many of us would go to a parade with one entry? And that one entry included a donkey! Not sure I would. And yet, here He is, and so are they. They have come to cheer for their king. Oh, He is their king, but it will not be in the way they thought. For now, there is only excitement, for now there is only praise, for now there is hope. It's no different today. Who do you see riding the donkey?

Is he a man, or is He God? Each of us has to decide. During this Easter season, why not join the parade as we celebrate Jesus. Get close enough so you can see your reflection in His eyes...because you need to know that what comes next, He did for you!

****

The Day after Palm Sunday

When it is cold outside, I do my walking inside our church, and today was no different. As I turned on the lights my eyes were drawn to the pile of palm branches lying on the altar. With every round that I walked I met up with them: lifeless palm branches. Yesterday they were being waved as children and adults marched around the church singing "Hosanna! Blessed is He who comes in the name of the Lord." Yesterday we were no different than the crowd that cheered for Jesus, and I realized that when I looked at the palm branches lying on the altar, that we are no different today than they were the day after they cheered for Jesus. They all went back to their normal lives, went to work, they resumed their daily tasks. Did they pause to reflect on what had happened yesterday? Do we? That they would forget so soon the shouts of praise for their King, and within days out of the same mouth we would hear crucify him! Would that be me? I know myself too well to say I would be any different. Case in point...I left my palm branch on the altar.

But as I continued to walk it became clearer to me.... isn't that just where Jesus would want us to leave them. That is where He meets us. So today I am glad my palm branch is on the altar. It is a reminder of where my life should be.... laid at His feet.

****

Easter Morning

As Mary approached the tomb that Easter morning, still engulfed with the grief of the past few days, she saw the stone rolled back. Not thinking about anything but Jesus and His missing body, I'm sure the sadness in her heart at that moment must have been overwhelming. She had just watched Him die and entombed; now His body is gone. She then asks the gardener, where is the body? Her only concern is Jesus, and He has been taken from her. Then, at the time she didn't think she could take any more, the man speaks. "Mary." It's all she needed to hear. It was Jesus. He is not dead! He is ALIVE! When we are at our deepest despair, listen. And you will hear Jesus call...He's ALIVE....and He knows your name.

****

Easter and April Fool's Day

I love reading all the "He is Risen" posts on Facebook. If you spend any time reading my posts, you know that Jesus and what He did for me is the most important part of my life. He changed me. No, I should say He is in the process of changing me for I am a work in progress. So today I too celebrate His resurrection. It is great being able to celebrate the resurrection with my family and friends. But I also can't forget today is April Fool's Day too. I come from a family that spent lots of time playing April Fool's Day jokes on each other. No one in our family was exempt from the jokes. From waking up with someone shouting, "It's snowing outside!" to my mom disabling my dad's car at his work parking lot to making chocolate-covered cotton balls to pass out in school, we were a creative bunch. Laughter rang throughout our house as we heard "April Fool's!" repeated over and over. So, I am loving that today is Easter, and smiling because I am reminiscing a simpler time in life where trying to fool someone was the most fun thing to do.

****

Thankful for Pastors

October is Pastor Appreciation month. I would like to thank the many Pastors who have influenced my faith walk over the years. I have known my share of Pastors, some good, some not, some with amazing sermons, some not, some with great people skills, some not, but what each one of these Pastors had in common was a love for Jesus that they were willing to spend their life telling others about Him. Looking back now each of them left an imprint on my life to help make me the person I am today. So, thank you for devoting your life to telling others about the saving love of Christ. I am a life that was changed. A personal note to Pastor Mike McCrumb: Thanks for putting up with me! You're the best.

****

Funerals and Friends

I attended a funeral today for a woman that had lived 95 years. She was my good friend's mother. The funeral was a celebration of life for sure, but it still came with the sadness of losing a loved one, even when you know they are finally at home enjoying eternal peace. As a spectator I watched a video that was played which highlighted the many moments of this woman's life. Seven minutes that tried to capture 95 years of living. As good as it was, it did not come close to capturing her life. Only her close friends and family were able to see between the photos and take pride in the life she lived. Only they can attest to the love she shared with them, to the joy they brought to her, and to the love she had for Jesus. As I looked at the shell that housed my friend's mother for 95 years, I was reminded how fleeting this thing called life is. Funerals do that to you. They remind us that life ends this way for all of us. It is also my nudge to love more, to make my days count, and to try to finish this race of life well. My friend's mom did just that. The love she lavished on others was not wasted, it was not lost. It was evident in those she left behind. They will carry with them every bit of the love that she gave them, for love never fails.

****

Note to self…After attending three funerals in one week

Not one person talked about what kind of car the deceased drove, or how big or small of a house they lived in, or even what kind of clothes they wore. Note to self: When tempted to compare material things with happiness…DON'T!

The memories that were shared were not from fancy vacations, or even required lots of money. Note to self: It's in the way I treat people every day and how I live my life that will create memories; see and treat others with love and kindness.

Laughter is universal, and it is understood by everyone. Note to self: Make someone smile every day.

A life lived for Christ is all that matters in death. Note to self: Live each day here on earth as it is my last.

****

Why Not Try Church?

Are you looking for a church in the area to attend? I realized that if you attend any churches (which there are many) in our community, you will be in attendance with people who are recovering from addictions of all kinds, from pornography to alcohol and drugs. You will also meet women who have had abortions, men and women who have gone through divorce, and you might run across some downright angry people. Now I'm sure you're asking yourself, why in the world would I want to be around people like that? You see, going to church is not about how perfect you are, it's all about how perfect Jesus is. Most of us attend church because we know how much we fail and are in need of saving. So why not join us this Sunday. You will be met by people just like you, and hopefully through them you will meet their Father who is full of forgiveness. We will be expecting you.

****

Family

What fun it has been to scroll through the many 4th of July family parties. I can tell from all the smiles and good pictures a great time was had by all. I can also say we had a great family fun pool party and picnic too, but even when my family is all together, there are still missing spots where members used to be. Even with all the laughter and joking there are people who are missed; if not openly, then in our hearts. They were not with us for many reasons. Some have died, some have divorced, some just had other commitments and couldn't be here. So, families adjust. We enjoy those who are with us, we miss those who aren't, and I'm sure we will make room for others who come. Can we ever stop being part of a family we once belonged to? I think not. A part of us always remains as we leave our touch on one family and in turn, we carry them with us. Family, what a great gift God has blessed us with! Cherish the one you have.

****

Why?

Do you ever have days where life hits you so hard that you have trouble even taking a breath? Today has been that day for me. It's not that I am going through any particular struggle in my life, but it seems that many in my family and friends circle are finding life pretty hard at this time. I could list the many struggles that are making life hard for those I love, but I'm sure it wouldn't be much different from the struggles in the lives of those you love. So, I wonder at times why does life have to be so hard. Why is it just as hard to watch those close to you suffer, as it is for us to go through the suffering ourselves? Then I remember, the times in my life that were the hardest became the times that I grew the most in my faith. They gave me the opportunity to help others going through the same things, to have a heart of compassion for others, and to know that God places people in our lives to help us through the tough times. I never thought I would say this, and I didn't say it in the midst of the struggle, but I thank God for my struggles. I am pretty sure I am a better person because of them.

****

Can you have real joy?

Yesterday I started out my Friday as usual with breakfast at a restaurant with friends, shopping with two friends for a few hours, and finishing the day shopping with Paul. It made for a fun filled day. Lots of laughter and memories were made. Christmas time is here. And then reality hit. Today, I know someone who is suffering grief from the loss of a loved one, and a young mom trying to find a place to live, with overwhelming difficulties. I know someone getting ready to make a decision today that will affect the rest of her life. So many heart aches, so much pain, and too much sorrow. How can I even begin to understand their struggles? How can I rejoice in the season when those close to me are hurting? Can I really experience the peace and joy of the season? Yes! It's because I know the baby in the manger. He was sent into the world for those who are hurting, for those looking for wisdom, for those who grieve, He was sent here for all of us. Everyone one of us will face days that will be hard to endure. Remember during the good times and bad times...the Gift of Christmas is for you! You just have to reach out to Him. It will be the best present you ever receive.

****

(The next few pages are a story that starts with a fall and ends standing.)

My mom's fall

Last Thursday my life was focused on helping to work at a Moose Lodge breakfast for The Women's Center, organizing our upcoming Life Walk, and going to baseball games and band concerts. In a moment, all of my plans were rearranged. My mom at 88 years young had fallen down the stairs of her home in Nashville TN. It's interesting how those things that you plan to do take an immediate back seat to the things that are most important. Our priorities can change in the blink of an eye. I think it took about an hour for my sister Sandy and I to get all of our plans changed and we headed south. My mother has a great group of friends and neighbors who watched out for her until we got to the hospital on Friday evening. Our hearts broke as we looked at our mom bruised, broken and full of pain...but she was alive. Who knows what the next weeks or months would bring? Who knows how we will figure out her care and healing between Michigan and Tennessee? Who knows what other plans will have to change? These are questions that will need to be answered soon, they are questions that God already knows the answers to but today is Mother's Day, and I (speaking for all my siblings) have a whole new appreciation for being able to say Happy Mother's Day Mom. We ask for prayers for her healing and for the many decisions that will have to be made, but today is Mother's Day and it will be spent at the hospital caring and serving mom. We are truly blessed.

Thank you for praying for my mom. Her surgery was a success, and we are looking forward to the healing process. She now has a metal plate with several screws holding her shoulder together...we have much to be thankful for....

Good news to our ears this morning. As we wondered just how this Nashville- Michigan rehab thing was going to work, God stepped in and seems to be making a way we did not even know about. Since mom is in relatively good health, she is quite possibly a candidate for the hospital rehab unit. This would mean she would be moved from the 7th floor to the 3rd floor in hospital rehab (relieving the thought of placing her in a rehab home we know nothing about). They would work solely on rehab for around 10 days. This would give us time to get home and then figure a way to retrieve her back to Michigan. They will also help set up continuing rehab if needed in Michigan. So much to be thankful for this morning!

We are watching your prayers being answered. After a discouraging evening of indecision this morning we were notified that mom will be moving to the rehab floor. This unit is four years old and has room for 20 patients. Thankfully, there is a room open for her. As we watched mom walk today from her bed to the bathroom to peek out into the hallway, it was the best gift we have received to this point. The verse in James states it perfectly: Every good and perfect gift is from above. We do not take them for granted! Thank you for joining us on this journey that we never wanted...but we are embracing what it is with thankful hearts.

Just an update for those who are wondering how our mom is doing. We were delightfully surprised that we were told she will be coming home May 31st. After many sleepless nights, stress-filled decision making, and a bruised and broken body, healing is taking place. Our bodies are amazing. To see her at 88 years young, have an incision already healing, her bruising starting to fade (a little), and her sense of humor return is just what her kids want to see. Many hurdles yet to cross but each day brings us closer to total healing! God is good, even when we don't feel it, when we question His plan and when we lose our cool. He is in control and He is good!

****

Mother's Day

At my age having my mom still here to celebrate with is something that I do not take for granted. I count it a blessing to still be able to pick up the phone and hear her voice. Sometimes her voice sounds a bit tired, sometimes I can hear pain in her voice but every time I call there is a gladness that speaks loud and clear as she listens to her baby. Yes, being the youngest of 6 kids, no matter how old I am, I'm still the baby. Today we talked and I asked her to pray for a specific need in my family and I realized that as a mom no matter how old you get, your heart breaks when your family hurts. Sharing my prayer concerns and knowing she will be on her knees for our family is probably the best Mother's Day gift I will receive this year. (I still expect the hanging flower baskets Steve and James.) So moms out there, I hope you will follow my mom's lead and pray for your families, that's where we all need to be.... on our knees!

****

Soccer Games and Grandkids

Lessons learned today at a five-year old's soccer game. No matter how they played, the crowd went wild. Keep kicking! Your feet will connect with the ball eventually and you will see a goal scored. When the ball comes to you in midair and you accidentally touch it, okay, you grab it with both hands, no one even cares, in fact the spectators all laugh. When you play hard, you get to take a break, get refreshed with a cool drink of water, and get high fives from your family. When the game is over there's treats for all! Why can't life be more like a five-year-old's soccer game?

****

Prayer Request Failure

A few weeks ago, a person I know was going through a rough time. She had to be at a court hearing and I said I would be praying for her. I even made a mental note of the time and vowed to pray for her. That day came and went without one thought of her or what she was going through, until she left a message that everything went great. I had failed. I felt terrible. Thankfully, God does not need me to carry out His plan, but He does expect me to keep my word. I said I would pray for her and I didn't. Ever find yourself feeling like you disappointed God? Well, that was just how I felt. I 'm sure I have done this in the past, and I am sure I'm not alone. So why did it hit me so hard on that day? Was God trying to get me to see what a failure I had been? No, He doesn't work that way. He did show me that when I say I am going to pray for someone I better do it because it makes me take the focus off of myself and be able to put that focus on someone in need. Will I fail again? Yes, but I am so glad that even before that day had passed, I was asked to pray for someone else. I smiled to myself as I thanked God for giving me another chance. And yes, I did pray!

****

Friends and Grief

This morning I have already enjoyed a good breakfast with friends, been able to reflect on my granddaughter's high school play last evening and have begun to process what the rest of my day will look like. Then it hit me, today is March 23. An ordinary day for most of us, but to one of my friends this day brings a reminder of great loss. In the process of going about my day today I am going to be more aware of the people I see who today might be having a difficult one. Maybe their smile won't be as big, maybe you will see a dullness in their eyes where a spark would usually reside, or maybe they just need to be alone with their memories. Whatever it might be, we need to be aware that a great day for us might be the worst day in someone else's life. So, I pray this morning for my friend, but I also pray that God would give me eyes to see others who are hurting and if I can do nothing else Lord, at least I can give them my smile.

****

God has a Sense of Humor

For those of you who have known me for a long time, you should get what I mean when I say God has a sense of humor. I know very well the attributes of God: Holy, Just, Truthful, and Loving to name a few, but sense of humor comes to mind every time I prepare for a Purity Weekend. He took a young girl of 17 who was pregnant, then later married and divorced and remarried, and He still said, I choose you to share my message of Purity through The Delton Women's Center. Now that's funny! And yet, here we are getting ready for our 20th session. We will meet with five moms and daughters, so after this weekend we will have shared with 100 girls God's plan of Purity for them. So today I am excited to share again what an awesome God we serve who not only loved me through the hard times, forgave me through my screw ups, but also joins me in laughter.

****

Christmas

Tomorrow is Christmas Eve. My day will start and end in church. Sandwiched in between we will have the family gathering at our house. There will be too much food, lots of laughter and of course a few presents to open. Some gifts will need to be returned, some will be loved, others just acceptable. I mean what kid really likes to get socks and a toothbrush? So, my day will be full, along with my heart. I only have to open my eyes to see the blessings that I have been granted. Don't think for a moment though that our lives have not been scarred by life. If we are breathing, we will all experience joy and sorrow as we walk through life. Many years ago, I received a gift that was perfect in every way. Perfect fit, perfect peace, perfect joy. It was the gift of Salvation. Free but not cheap. So, I'm looking forward to tomorrow, when my day will start and end with Jesus, thanking Him for His gift. Tomorrow I will be thankful for His gift, and that not only tomorrow, but that every day I am granted starts and ends In Christ. Merry Christmas.

****

The Yellow Brick Road

Facebook asks, "What's on your mind?" Today I was thinking about The Wizard of Oz! How's that for a crazy thing to think! My granddaughter will be in her school's production this spring, and my mind was on the path of "The Yellow Brick Road." When I was a kid, I couldn't believe that Dorothy and Toto followed that road, stayed on the path with all kinds of crazy obstacles in their way only to finally get to the wizard who was a fake! What a letdown....it was just a man behind the curtain! Really?

You take on the witch, the lion, the scarecrow and a tin man, oh and not forgetting the flying monkeys, and the munchkins when you finally get to a man turning knobs behind a curtain. Who has no power at all! Seriously! That just stinks. Isn't that a lot like life though? We think we are on a path that leads home, only to find the path we are on is fake. We are skipping our way down a yellow brick road that leads to nothing but hopeless trouble. So today, I would encourage you to examine the path you are strolling down. The color of the road is unimportant, but you need to make sure who you are following and just what home it will lead you to. I'm choosing to follow Christ; I sure hope to see you along the way! And for gosh sakes, I hope there are no flying monkeys...they just creeped me out!

****

New Year

I just received a reminder on Facebook that in two days it will be 2018! Wow, who knew? Glad they let me know. I can now look back to see 2017 for what it was: a year filled with much laughter, some disappointments, good health, and much thankfulness. I like to look back.

The times that I worried too much about the things I had no control over turned out just fine. So, I learned to trust again. The times that my heart was so full of love I thought it would burst. I learned again it comes from the One who is love. Oh, and there were those hard times when my soul cried out in pain from lost loved ones, injustice, and rampant evil in this world. It was here that I learned to be comforted by the Great Comforter. So, as I look ahead to 2018 not knowing what it will bring, I'm sure I will have to learn these lessons all over again. I'm not a quick learner. I'm sure I will fail many of the trials set before me in 2018, but that's okay too, because thankfully Jesus is not only trustworthy, full of love, the Great Comforter, He is also loaded with PATIENCE!!! Happy New Year!

****

Looking Back

As I scroll the Facebook posts on the last day of 2018, I am encouraged by some, discouraged by others and some are just downright unbelievable. There are the posts that are sad but end up happy, there are the political posts that no matter where you fall in that spectrum you will be disliked, and the posts of the ones who are thankful that 2018 is over. I guess that sums up life for us in 2018. Sad, happy, keep your opinions to yourself, and hold on - it will be over soon. I manage to float in and out of each of these categories as I am hit with different circumstances. My emotions often get the best of me. Whether I am flying high with excitement, or in the midst of anger, or just plain disgusted at life, what I know for a fact is God is in control.

In spite of my emotional roller coaster, His love remains the same. In spite of my loss of control, He never loses His. And in spite of not being sure what 2019 will bring, I don't have to worry; He is already there.

****

Praying Together

Sometimes I get a few words going through my head that just don't leave me alone. The phrase for yesterday and all day today is "The family that prays together stays together." I know that sounds great, and I do think quite often it is true, but not always. Families do not always stay together, even if they pray together. I have seen it happen many times. Yesterday, my brother-in-law had a serious fall and was airlifted to a hospital and thankfully is okay. Entering his room in the ER we were met by several other family members. We watched as the medical personnel did their jobs and we all breathed a sigh of relief when they said he would be okay. Not right away, but he would heal. As we were getting ready to leave, the family gathered around him and thanked God for His protection, His strength and

His peace. It was that moment that the words rang in my head. It's not that this family was praying together so we could stay together, it was that they were praying. Each one of us knows Who to go to during times of need and times of plenty. So, in the end, the best and most important part of that phrase is "The family that prays".... then no matter what happens we will be right where we need to be...in God's hands.

****

Expiration Dates and Friends

Just when did we start putting expiration dates on things? I don't remember it as a kid, but then there was never a time we ever had much food left over to expire. Last week I attended the funeral of a friend who had been at one time a close friend. Then life moved us in different directions. When our paths did cross, we would ask each other how we were doing, how our families were, and how time was flying by so fast. Then we would be on our way. I can't remember the exact time I last saw him, but today I was thinking that if he had an expiration date stamped on him, I know I would have taken more time to find out how he really was. Not just casual talk. If the moment we were born we could see an expiration date somewhere on us...would we be more caring, understanding and loving? Why didn't God just tattoo it on us? I am sure that would lead to many other issues.... but maybe for a minute we would see each other as God sees us...with love. Oh, I have such a long way to go...

****

Christmas

Today I read the Christmas story from Luke. Before I started reading it, the phrase "what do you do with the baby," kept going through my mind. As I was reading, those words became my focus. To Mary, a young unwed virgin, the baby meant big problems in the culture she lived, but she said "yes" to the baby, and Joseph, the adopted father of Jesus, also not understanding, said "yes".

The wise men from afar traveled a long distance to say "yes" to this baby. Shepherds in the fields sought out this baby and said "yes". What I had a hard time wrapping my mind around today was

Simeon and Anna. They saw Jesus being brought to the temple and they said "yes" to this baby. What made this baby any different from all the other babies brought to the temple? What stood out about Jesus from all the other babies? Many people were at the temple and I'm sure they saw Jesus as just another baby. So, what was it? Simeon and Anna knew He was the One that would bring salvation to the people. It's no different today. Some see the baby Jesus as just a baby, while others see him as the Savior. So, I guess each of us has to ask.... what will I do with the baby Jesus? Is he Savior or just another baby? The choice has been the same for 2,000 years. Choose wisely.

****

Prayer

Question for the day: when you pray is it mostly to petition God? You know how to tell Him what you need, what you want for others, then you give Him advice on how to handle the situation you're in. Yeah, that's me. But today along with the word petition, the word listen came to mind. I have to admit I'm not that good at it when I'm talking to God. Yet how can I really have a relationship if I'm always the one doing the talking? I can guarantee you God already knows exactly what I am going to say, but He patiently listens. I, on the other hand, have absolutely no way of knowing what He wants from me or for me if I don't take the time to listen to Him. There is a reason He says, "Be still and know that I am God". Today I am trying to be still and hear His voice. How about you? Will you petition or listen? How about doing both!

****

Men and Integrity

As I woke up this morning to the continuing unfolding story of Harvey W on the news and the growing list of "me too" on social media, my heart is sick. For all the women who have been disrespected in the workplace, for those abused, for those living in fear and being too scared to speak up, we as a society should be ashamed. But then I am remembering a few weeks ago when this same society gave honor to Hugh Hefner. We glorify books like <u>Fifty Shades of Gray,</u> and we have a multibillion dollar pornography industry that is growing daily. So, then I ask myself, should we really be surprised when people act out what they see glorified all around them? I know it would be easy to become suspect of all men, but I also know there are men who choose to live lives of integrity and today I am going to focus on them. Thank you for your respect of women, for working hard, and for being great husbands, fathers and sons. Paul Hughes, Neil Hughes, Dale Campbell Sr., Steven Norris and James Norris, God has blessed me through each of you.

****

Children's Sermon

As I was reading today in Matthew 11, I was once again reminded of a children's sermon that I had shared during a Sunday service a few years ago. The kids were seated around me and I had a large back pack that was loaded with very heavy books. I asked my oldest grandson Lincoln to put on the backpack and start carrying it around the church while I was reading Matthew 11:28-30. We watched him take off as he started his journey. After a few times around the church, the weight of the backpack was starting to get to him, so after the 3rd time around I removed a few of the books. Not all of them, just a few. And off he went. A bit lighter but still weighed down, and after a few more circles around the church with a very heavy load, he became weary of the burden. So again, I removed a few more books. This happened until every book was unloaded from the pack and he could easily make his way without being weighed down. Are you familiar with words, "Come to me, all you who are weary and burdened, and I will give you rest?" Do you feel like the load you carry is way too heavy for you? Are you overwhelmed with the trials of this out of control world? Are you weighed down with past regrets? I know that I often try to carry a load that was never meant for me to carry. I must give it all to Jesus, ALL of it. For when I keep some for myself, I soon end up again being overloaded and weighted down with the problems before me. Rest...Jesus says if we come to Him...that is what we get...I am all about that. How about you?

****

Peace

I woke this morning with a sense of overwhelming sadness, and this is so not me. But today even before my feet hit the floor there was this feeling of sadness that I have not been able to shake.

Scrolling Facebook seems to add to the sadness I feel. Let's see, a family member who is going through the loss of an in-law, fighting on Facebook posts of who is right or wrong in building a wall, what news media outlet speaks truth, politicians who we vote to represent us, yet live so far above us that they have no clue, the government shut down, and the one that tips the scale to overload for me...New York, along with many other states giving women the right to kill their children up to the point of delivery. I am sorry to see what our country has become. The pain, the anger, the outright hatred for others is not how we should live. Thankfully in all my sadness I serve a God who whispers to me, I AM.

****

Who I am in Christ

For a few weeks now the phrase, "Mirror, Mirror on the Wall, Who is the fairest of them all," has been floating across my mind at different times. Not really knowing why and trying to understand the lingering phrase...here I write. Most of you, like me have heard the story of the princess who was the fairest in all the land. I was always fascinated with the talking mirror, and also more intrigued with the wicked witch who wanted to be the fairest of all, and it was never going to be her. She was the bad witch after all.

A mirror! Can we pass by them without stealing a glance at ourselves? As a young girl of 5, my mirror reflected a smile of who I was, but I didn't have much time to look at the reflection. There were just too many other things to do than to stare at myself in a mirror. Oh, but when I became a teenager the mirror became my best friend. Having 8 people in our family and 1 bathroom, my sister and I primped in our bedroom. We had a dressing table and on the table was a portable mirror...with lights all around it. Just like the movie stars. And we spent hours in front of that mirror. But not once did I ever look into that mirror and think that I was the fairest of them all. Many other girls had better skin, better hair, and better clothes. I was never going to reach that perfect person. Looking into the mirror as a young mom found a more mature girl, with responsibilities beyond her age looking back. Oh, the look of youth was still there, but I could see deeper into the eyes staring back at me that my life was changing. I was now responsible for two other little lives and the looks into the mirror were then just hit and miss. There were more important things to tend to. The mirror in my hand at times saw tears, the mirror at times saw joy, and yes, many times the mirror reflected the wicked witch. And now that mirror in my life shows a woman on "The Gray Side," still knowing she is never going to be the fairest of them all, and that's okay. Because now when I glance in the mirror, I think I see a little of my Father staring back at me. My Father, Jesus. And really in His mirror, I am the fairest of them all.

****

Life

As I was browsing Facebook a video caught my eye of a young woman who lost her battle with cancer at the age of 27. She had left her family and friends an extensive letter on life. She wanted to live. With everything that was in her, she was fighting a battle she knew she would not win. She wanted to marry, have children, grow old. Dying at 27 was not in her plans. It left me with a sadness in my heart. I know the many things I have taken for granted in this life. Those times I have squandered the precious minutes loaned to me flashed through my mind. Then I scrolled a bit further down the page and read an article about a fashion designer who at 55 took her life...that too left me with a sad soul. Two women, from two different walks of life, one fighting for life, one fighting to escape life, how does that happen? Try as hard as I might I can't wrap my mind around either situation. So, as I struggle with these situations, I realize that the only way I can find any sense in them is that I know Jesus never leaves those that reach out to Him. We all will face our mortality someday. Most of us have no clue when or how. I am praying you will make sure Jesus walks with you through it. You just need to ask Him.

****

Sun Rise, Son Shine

Morning at the lake is the time my soul is refreshed. Oh, I like anytime at the lake, but I have to say morning is my favorite. Before the sun comes up, the lake is gray and still. I am able to breathe in the peace that is all around. Then, slowly, the sun rises up enough to cast its glow on the surface of the water and the lake that was gray moments before responds with a brilliance that can't be described. It becomes a million diamonds dancing, it becomes a bright array of shimmering lights, it wakes up to the sun. The lake does nothing to contribute to the scene being played out before me. It is responding to the actions of the sun. The beauty set before me is a reminder of my life. There is nothing special about me until "The Son" shines His light on me. I do nothing to make this happen, but when He shines His light on me, I can do nothing less than reflect His peace, His beauty and His light. The sun on the lake will continue to rise, and the lake will remain a place of peace and quiet for me. But for those few moments in the morning, it shines in all its glory for the sun. I hope you allow the Creator to shine on you today. You will be amazed at what a little Son shine will do.

****

Discipline

The word floating around in my head this morning is discipline. It has been tossed around with a mixture of scenes playing out in my mind since Sunday when our Pastor talked about it...a loving father disciplines his children. I get that. We discipline and correct our children when they are behaving badly, in danger, or in need of a reminder of who is in charge. I get it, God, you discipline and correct me for the same reasons, .and quite often, well most of the time, I act just like a child getting disciplined. I don't like it. I can pout with the best of them, I can stomp my feet in anger, I can shake my fist and lose my temper and yet, I know You are in control, You know what is best for me and I am thankful that you love me enough to correct me!!!!

(Hebrews 12:6) check it out.

****

9-11

Everyone seems to know what happened that day. I too could tell you exactly what I was doing, and how I heard about the awful tragedy in our nation. I could tell you how my heart sank into my stomach as I watched in horror the two buildings coming down, realizing the loss of life that I was watching before my eyes. I could tell you about the news coverage and seeing the devastation in our country. I could tell you all those things, but you all know it too. Yet, in those moments our country changed from the innocence of peace to the realization of war. And we came together as a country. I watched as our leaders in Washington sang "God Bless America" together. I saw on every sign and in every city the words God Bless America, as men and women had flags flying from their car windows. In those moments we were a country united. United by everything that we hold dear: our country, our people and our freedoms. Yes, it seems the greatest tragedy we have experienced in our country also brought about the greatest unity too. Those days after 9-11 are hard to remember, but I will never forget the feeling of pride we had in our country. It wasn't them versus us...it was US...people of The United States of America doing what we do best. Helping, caring, loving, the best that we can. I wish that for us again. I just don't want to have it as a result of another tragedy. So, I will say with all my heart what we heard over and over 17 years ago.... God bless America. Help us never forget.

****

Imperfect family

There it is. The post on Facebook that is real. When you scroll Facebook pages you can easily get the idea that the families you see are perfect. They are always taking their kids places, they are always smiling and they are always wearing the right clothes, driving the perfect car, and of course they eat all the right foods. A person could get a warped sense of life if you just see the smiling, perfect times. Then I saw the post today that not only spoke to real life problems, but also had a request for prayer attached to it. Thank you, Melody I., for sharing your heart with us today. No one has perfect lives in spite of trying to look that way; we all have heartache and sorrow. I will pray for your son; he is in God's hands, and I can't think of a better place for him to be.

Signed......by a friend whose family is far from perfect, but serving a God who is!

****

Children's Sermon ahead...

A few years ago, we traveled to the West Coast. Like most tourists we collected information on interesting sights you want to see. One of the places on our list was Mount St. Helens. We had

91

looked at photos of it, we had mapped out our plan to see it, and we were on our way. The drive up to the mountain was beautiful, for a while anyway. The higher in elevation we went, the more the clouds rolled in, the misty rain dotted our windshield, and soon the scenery was gone. We were in the clouds, nothing to be seen, except the road in front of us. But we kept going. We wanted to see Mount St. Helens. Finally, we arrived at the top...and we saw nothing. Nothing. So, was it really there? We did not see it. We were right where they told us it would be, and it was not there. As far as Paul and I could tell, there was no Mount St. Helens. I pondered our dilemma on the way down the mountain. I am pretty sure if we asked the people in that area if Mount. St. Helens was there, they would say yes, and give me directions on how to get there, and they could tell me just what it looks like. And they would be right. We knew it was there, it was probably close enough for us to touch it, but we didn't see it. I know many out there have thought about God this way. You don't see Him; therefore He is not there. What you don't know is, just like Mount. St. Helens, He is there, others will tell you about Him, others will describe Him to you, but you must see Him for yourself. Just like we had a map to get us to the mountain top, God has left us one too. Why not check it out? I wouldn't want you to miss finding Him.

****

Christmas

Christmas is just a few days away and I am getting those last minute gifts wrapped, the menu for the meals to come planned and reflecting on the past year. Some things this past year have brought so much joy. As a grandma, anything your grandkids are involved in is fun: watching band concerts, plays and of course the many sports activities. Whether they win or lose, who really cares? We have welcomed new babies into the family, had battles with cancer, death and divorce. I have a feeling that many of you have walked the same path with your families too. I am realizing the older I get that life is not fair, life is not always a walk in the park, but life is always a blessing. It must be lived to the fullest. So, as you embark on the New Year, know that struggles will come, but they will be mixed in with many blessings along the way. Take the time to count them. God sends them to us as His reminder of His love for us. So, have a

Merry Christmas and be watching for those blessings, you don't want to miss them.

****

Gifts

I am sitting here in front of a pile of gifts that need to be wrapped, each gift chosen for someone I love. I will wrap until my back hurts, then wrap some more. Sometimes I find myself laughing as I wrap the gifts thinking of the expression on the face of the receiver as they open the gift.

Giving. It is what this season is all about. In order to give, though, we have to have a receiver. God gave us the gift of Jesus. Like all gifts it is given freely, but it was not cheap. So, I wonder if God waits and laughs as He anticipates our reaction to His gift. Does He think about the look on our faces as we invite Him in? Does His heart fill with joy as we receive the perfect gift of His Son? I think it does. Wishing all my friends the best gift of all…Jesus.

Merry Christmas to each of you.

****

It is Christmas Eve.

I have already been blessed today by having my mom, my siblings and their spouses over today. We shared breakfast, laughter, a few tears and lots of reminiscing of days gone by. No more rushing today: gifts are wrapped, table reset for tomorrow and I am enjoying some quiet time. I am reminded today that in my joy of Christmas many that I know are having a hard time experiencing that joy. Cancer, death, and broken relationships are just a few reasons their joy has been robbed. As we look into the manger and see the gift of Jesus and his surroundings at birth, we see a smelly, dirty and lonely place. Jesus has come to us no matter what place or situation we find ourselves in. My prayer for those of you who are hurting is that you will be comforted by the peace that only He can bring. Hang on, you are not alone.

****

The Old Hymnal

Today as I went about my task of cleaning, I stumbled across a church hymnal. Since my husband plays piano, we have a few lying around. I was going to dust the cover and return it to its place on a shelf, but instead I opened it. As I thumbed through the pages of songs so many memories came to mind. I could hear my father singing "How Great Thou Art", and I remembered singing "Rock of Ages" at my uncle's funeral. As I turned more pages, more memories came. "Wonderful Grace of Jesus", a favorite of my friend's mom. I remembered Thanksgiving services as we sang "We Gather Together to ask the Lord's Blessings" and many candlelight Christmas Eve services as we sang "Silent Night". There were also songs that brought memories from sad times in my life, when I couldn't get through singing "In His Time" without tears streaming down my face. I literally walked through my past as I turned the pages of that hymn book. In today's world the hymnal is sometimes seen as outdated. Don't get me wrong, I love praise and worship songs, but I am feeling a little sad that many children today won't hear the hymns that our parents and grandparents grew up with. I guess they will have their own memories of songs to pass on, as the song says, In His Time, He makes all things beautiful.

****

Evil versus love for one another

As I scroll down Facebook and read the many comments posted on the Orlando shootings, I am finding it hard to wrap my mind around the horrible tragedy. I keep telling myself we live in a civilized society, but as I watch the news, I am brought to the realization that this might not be true anymore. And then as I watch this tragedy unfold, I see glimpses of humankind at its best. From those survivors inside the club, to first responders and the medical personnel, to those who formed a line to give blood. You are all showing us that true love for our brother comes from being willing to lay down our life for them. That compassion and kindness and love for one another is what truly matters. As a Christ follower this is what my life should reflect daily. Lord, help us to value life.

****

Does evil exist? What does it look like?

Questions you no doubt have heard asked before. But this past weekend in Kalamazoo we witnessed evil. Evil acts of randomly shooting innocent people for no reason? I will never understand how or why someone would want to harm anyone, yet we live in a culture where life seems to have no value. How did we get here? And how do we change it? I am reminded of a verse in Romans 12:21 "Do not be overcome by evil but overcome evil with good." Each of us has a part in either letting evil overcome us or doing good to overcome evil. The choice is yours; what will you do?

****

Divorce

Last Sunday, our Pastor Mike McCrumb delivered a difficult sermon on divorce. This was my letter to him in response: Just wanted to say thank you for the sermon on divorce. I can't begin to imagine how hard it was to preach. Those of us who have been divorced understand why God says don't do it. It was by far the most painful thing I have ever been through. It affects the whole family; it tears apart what was never meant to be apart and it leaves broken people in its path. Broken people who then try to find healing in many ways, but if our healing does not come through Christ, we start the whole mess again. Divorce is a killer: a killer of dreams, a killer of spirits, a killer of unity. Who wants that? Thankfully by God's grace we are able to pick up and move on and in His great love for us, He allows us happiness and joy again. Praise be to God.

****

Red Rover, Red Rover, send_____right over! You fill in the blank.

What comes to your mind when you hear that saying? Maybe nothing. But if you are over the age of 50, an image of 2 lines of kids holding hands in gym class, while facing each other might appear in your mind. One team shouts out the Red Rover saying, and soon the person whose name is called out is running as fast as they can to break through the opposite line of kids. Why on earth is that going through my mind today? Well, in a Bible Study group I am in, we are learning about the Armor of God. I found it interesting that Roman soldiers would stand locked together, arm in arm, feet pressed firm into the ground accompanied with studs on the bottom of their shoes to hold them firmly in place. While I was studying the scene of the soldier, the Red Rover game popped into my mind. No matter what age I am, focus is always hard for me. But this time Red Rover seemed to bring an object lesson. For one thing, in school, we held hands with our team mates as hard as we could, trying not to be the weakest link when the opposition came charging at us. Alas, it was to no avail, they would always break through. When that happened, they took the weakest link back to their group. This played out until one team had managed to capture all the opposite team members. Roman soldiers did not stand holding hands in a line, they locked arm in arm (hmm… why didn't we do this?)...they planted their feet firmly in the ground (this would have been good too)...they held their shield in front of their breastplate...and they moved forward together. The lines of soldiers were a line that could not be penetrated. They needed each other.   If one was weaker, the two on either side would hold them up. As I study the Armor of God, and I put on my armor as commanded, it helps to protect me. It gives me protection from the enemy, and as I lock arms with my Christian brothers and sisters, it makes us strong. We will be a force that cannot be moved. Interested in The Armor of God, check it out in Ephesians 6:10-19. Just wondering...do kids still play Red Rover?

****

Baptism and Fathers

Yesterday I attended a baptism of a girl young in age, but wise in faith. Apparently, she had wanted to be baptized for quite a while and her father, wanting to make sure she understood all about baptism, set out to teach her. During that time, her desire to be baptized never changed. As many of us stood watching this precious moment, she bravely walked out into the water. Right beside her was her Pastor. As she prepared to go under the water, tears filled her eyes, not tears of fear, but tears of joy. Then in the name of the Father, Son and Holy Spirit she was baptized. The picture that will remain in my mind for a very long time was seeing her come out of the water. In an instant, she wrapped herself in her Pastor's arms and held tight. Her Pastor with big arms and a big heart hugged this little girl with all he had in him. I am pretty sure at that time there were tears in all of our eyes...it was the perfect picture of the love Jesus has for us. For you see, the Pastor was not only her Pastor but her father too. And the love of a father for his precious child reminded me just how precious we are to Jesus. What a beautiful day!

****

The Well and a Ledge

I have had this story floating around in my mind for the last couple of weeks, not sure why, and not sure if I should share it. But it won't leave me, so maybe if I put it into words it will quit hanging around. If you have known me very long, you know that I was married at 17. Before I graduated high school, I was a Mrs. and soon to be a mom. We lived in a small house on Crooked Lake. It was our first home and I was pretty excited about it. In the early spring of that year, I was eager to get the yard cleaned up, so I set out to do some raking while my husband was at work. It was still pretty chilly out and I remember putting on my winter coat, one that would fit over my growing belly. I started to rake leaves off of the new grass showing in the yard. It wasn't too long before I shed that coat; I was working up quite a sweat. Then as I continued to rake, in an instant the ground under me gave way and I was falling. At this point I wish I could say I cried out to God. I didn't. I remember saying oh sh**! I was covered in old water and sludge and I wasn't sure how I was going to get out of this deep hole I was in. Thankfully, I had removed that heavy winter coat moments before. This all happened in a blink of an eye, but I remember grabbing a ledge and pulling myself out. I was a mess, I was scared, I was not sure if my baby was okay. I got into the shower and cried. We had no phone and only one car, so I waited for my husband to get home a few hours later. After explaining to him what happened, he went out to find that I had fallen into an old cistern whose cover had rotted and when I stepped on it, it gave way and I went straight down. He came back in and with a puzzled look on his face asked me how I ever got out? I told him I had grabbed onto the ledge and pulled myself up. He walked me out to the hole and told me to look. There were no ledges at all in that hole. I know when I fell and reached up there was a ledge. I also know without a doubt that God, with Whom nothing is impossible, created a ledge for me and rescued me from what could have been a very different ending. I am not sure why I have been reliving that story from so long ago. 45 years have passed since then. And yet, when I remember that day, I can say without a doubt that if you are in the pit, reach up.   He created a ledge for me; just imagine what He can do for you.

****

Community Outdoor Worship

After a day of reflection, I am ready to put into words what my heart was feeling yesterday. A beautiful sunrise with a slight coolness to the morning air gave way to an anticipation of what

God would do at our second Community of Faith Celebration. He did not disappoint. How often do you hear of several different churches gathering together for Sunday morning worship? Sad to say, not too often. For those of us in Delton who attended the service yesterday we are among those who experienced a bit of what I think heaven will be like. Our focus was not on the music, yet it was awesome, it was not on those who read Scripture, and that was amazing, it was not on the children who sang for us, or the soloists who blessed us with their talents It was on the One who is worthy of our worship. Jesus. And we worshipped. Outside where we could see the beauty of His creation, outside where we as Christ followers shared our common love, outside where no walls could contain the love, we have for Him, for our community and for each other. It was outside where an eagle flew with wings wide open as we sang "How great is our God." Words cannot describe the beauty of that moment. My mind is already starting to think about next years' service, but today I am going to cherish the beauty of yesterday's worship, and what a special time it was....as I sing in my heart.... How Great is Our God!

****

Longevity and Loneliness

Many of you know about my mom's fall in May, that she is staying in Delton and trying to get better. She will be 89 in October and we are so thankful that she is still here to be part of our lives. I have been trying to understand how she must feel from day to day. It's not that she doesn't enjoy all of her kids, I know she does. And yet, there has been a sadness in her eyes lately that is hard to miss.

The downside of living as long as she has is having to say goodbye to so many close friends and family. One of her close friends passed away a few days ago, and a beloved sister-in-law is under hospice care at this time. So again, she prepares to say another goodbye. How many more will she say? Only God knows. As I try to see through her eyes I am reminded of my friends, and how I will react when I have to start saying goodbye. The day might come when I look around and my circle of friends is no longer a circle, but a place where only one stands. I don't like to even think about it, but for my mom it is a reality every day. So, we will all try to get that twinkle back in my mom's eyes again. She knows deep down it's not really goodbye, but rather a See You Later.

That is what Jesus has promised. For now, her heart aches, and so does ours. Life can be so hard.

****

What is your heart's desire?

Trust me, those are not the thoughts I usually wake up to! Yet it was there, and I have been tossing it over in my mind since then. What are the desires of your heart? I guess it is something all of us should know, or at least think about. I could tell you many things my heart desires. Most are good things- you know, those things that all of us want. And then it hit me...want. Are those things I want really what my heart desires? In Psalm 37, it tells me to delight in the Lord and He will give me the desires of my heart. So, when I spend time with Jesus, does He change my heart to desire His wants? When I start listening to Him more, do MY wants become less and HIS desires become more, so that soon there is only His desire in my heart? I know this is true, and yet my selfish desires creep in often. I am sure that is the reason I woke to the thought, what is your heart's desire? How about you? What does your heart desire today? Spend some time delighting in The Lord and let Him show you what your heart truly desires...I know I plan to.

****

New Year, Old Knee

Well, I didn't realize I would be reflecting so soon on my words 3 days ago. Knowing that God would meet me in 2019 was comforting then but even more so today. I consider myself fairly active, walking, stair climbing, along with other daily routines keep me busy. But when my feet hit the floor yesterday morning I felt a pain in my leg that I knew wasn't right. Something was definitely wrong. So, being pretty sure it was a pulled muscle but also finding it very difficult to get around I made the decision to go to an Urgent Care. After getting some x-rays the doctor told me my knee was a mess (my words, not hers). There was talk about lots of swelling, not much cushion between joints and possible knee replacement. My response was, after the deer in the headlight look, you have got to be kidding me! So here I am today reclining in my chair, leg elevated and braced thinking about all the things I need to do. I am not telling you this for sympathy, because in the big scheme of life it ranks pretty low, but knowing that God knows what my 2019 looks like, that He listens to my whining about all the things going undone, and yet, in His still small voice He reminds me.....I got this!!! That's all I really need to know!

****

One drop of blood.

I had the TV on while cooking in the kitchen today. (I know it's hard to believe but I do cook sometimes!) A movie was on that made the observation how much you can tell about a person with one drop of blood. As I pondered that statement, the person went on to say that you can find out eye color, hair color, ethnicity, male, female, all from one drop of blood. There is almost nothing you can't find out about a person from one drop of his or her blood. Except.....WHAT kind of person they are. Are they kind? Doesn't show up in the drop of blood. Are they compassionate? Can't tell that either. Grumpy, cranky, nice, or sensitive? Are they faithful, do they have integrity? None of the real important stuff shows in the blood. Not sure why it hit me today, but if you believe that Jesus died for you, by shedding His blood to cover you, it has to result in His qualities flowing through us. So even though one drop of my blood will tell you many things about me, Jesus' blood covering me should also tell His story and reflect His qualities in me too. Oh, do I have a long way to go....so glad He has lots of patience.

****

Beauty between the weeds

This year I haven't had time to weed my flower beds. They just have not ranked very high on my priority list. So, as I would sit on my porch and watch the flowers come up, all I could do was focus on the weeds that were everywhere. Until today. My mom was over and we sat on the porch together. She admired every flower that was there. I thought to myself does she not see all the weeds? I sure did. But her focus was on the beauty of the flowers. She admired all of them, checking out the colors, the size, the different types. She saw the beauty! Life is so much like my flower gardens. When you stop focusing on the problems in your life you might be surprised at the beauty you will see everywhere! Thank you, God, for teaching me a life lesson today, and thanks to my mom for helping me see the beauty! The blessing today was mine.

****

Dreams

Not sure how many of you have dreams, but I have them often. Some are vivid and stick with me for days, some are funny and I find myself laughing, and sometimes I have ones that are fearful. Last night I had one full of fear. I would wake up hoping to get out of the dream, and drift back to sleep again, only to join the very same dream, or should I say the same fear. I can feel the sadness, I am overwhelmed with the situation that I find myself in. It is a fear that I carry in my sub-conscious mind. It is one I will probably never have to face again, but one I did live in my past. This morning as I am still feeling the sting of my dream, I am also in the midst of the reality that the thing I fear does not have its anchor in my daily life. I know that God calls me not to fear; I get it when I am awake, but not when I sleep. I want to be able to say in the deepest part of my soul, whether awake or asleep, the words of Isaiah 41:10..."So do not fear, for I am with you";...this morning my heart is still trying to calm down from a dream that seemed so real, but in reality has absolutely no truth in my life. Tonight in my dreams, I hope to laugh!!!!

****

101

Homecoming

I have been browsing Facebook posts and I happened on a site that shares videos of returning soldiers as they show up in varied places to surprise their kids. My heart gets excited to see the look of amazement on the kids' faces. A parent that they have not seen for a long time comes home. Usually there are tears, lots of hugs and a tangible scene of love that you are a witness to. You can get lost in the sight of love that is set before you, and you can almost feel the raw emotion between the two. This usually takes place with many others looking on. What I have noticed is the on-lookers stay as on-lookers. There is no move toward the returning soldier; there is joy on their faces, but the hug is reserved for the child. Isn't that just like God, to show us an example of His love through earthly pictures? No wonder we love to watch the video of the surprise return. Someday, and I am not sure when, God is going to walk in the door and I will see Him, and rush to Him. My eyes will fill with tears as His arms reach out to embrace me, and I will fall into this scene of love. Many others will look on, it is not their reunion, it will be mine. And to be honest with you, falling in His arms is something that I long to do. How about you?

****

Who is in your boat?

Can life get any crazier? Now restaurants are being asked to close! Let's see: school is closed, churches are closing, workplaces are empty and those whose jobs allow it are working from home. We are in the midst of living life like it has never been lived in recent times. It seems we are being rocked back and forth in waves of directives from our Government. Do this, don't do that, stay home, don't go out...back and forth the winds blow us. Scanning my Bible this morning, I was skimming over some of Jesus' teachings, and I was stopped in an instant as I read the sub title of Mark 4:35. Jesus calms the storm. I feel a bit like the disciples must have felt being in a boat that was being tossed to and fro in the midst of a wild sea. Waves were sweeping over the boat. I can imagine the disciples trying to bail out the water, all the time knowing that Jesus was asleep on the boat. Asleep, during all the fury of a storm, Jesus was there resting. It didn't take long for the disciples to wake him and ask, "Teacher, don't you care if we drown?" He got up and spoke to the wind and waves, "Quiet! Be still!" And they obeyed. Then Jesus asked his disciples why they were so fearful? Did they not have faith? Their response? They were terrified and asked each other, "Who is this, even the wind and the waves obey him?" In all our fears about this virus, in our rocking back and forth between the waves of uncertainty, guess who is in our corner? No longer in an earthly body needing sleep, but wide awake and in full control. Just like He was on that boat so long ago. The storm around us may be raging, but not if we know Jesus...He has been known to calm many storms. This one is not new to Him.

****

Eagles and Peace

Yesterday as I was driving home on Delton Road, I noticed that the car in front of me was slowing down and was looking off into a vacant field. He began to pull over, so of course that got my attention and I glanced out at the field too as I pulled my car off to the side, and the car behind me had pulled over. Three cars stopped alongside the road staring at a bald eagle which was sitting in the center of the field. I think all of us had our phones out to capture this beautiful bird. We watched this bird who had no cares in the world take a break in the middle of the field. For a brief moment in time just watching him gave me a peace and calmness. My day had been hurried and rushed, like I tend to make most of my days, but taking a moment to stop and give thanks to God for the chance to see this sight before me, well it was exactly what I needed. And if I could figure out how to get the picture of it off my phone and on this page, I would share it with you. Instead I will leave you with the verse that came to mind when I saw the eagle.

Check it out for yourself...Isaiah 40:31.

****

A Story of Forgiveness

Last night was the final session of a six-week Bible Study I have been attending at our church. It was on David. King David, a man after God's own heart, a strong and feared warrior, killer of the giant. I am sure you may have heard of him. His life seemed to have everything going for him and yet his life was also filled with screw ups and temptations. He also knew God. I was struck by that. He knew God, and he still gave into the temptations of his flesh. Let's see, there was the adultery with Bathsheba, which resulted in a pregnancy, and his intricate plan to have her husband killed to name a few. After Nathan, the prophet confronted him of his sins, he realized just how much he had sinned against God. Oh, his sin affected many others, but he knew that in the end, it was God who he sinned against. His heart was sick with what he had done. Did he wonder if God would forgive him? When he was broken in spirit from the weight of his sin, he asked for forgiveness...and... God forgave him. Oh, he still had severe consequences to pay. Sin always has them. What I realized about David during this study is that he did not let his screw ups stop him from continuing on the path that God had set for him. He could have done the, "Woe is me" and, "Why did I do that?" scenario for the rest of his days, and been no good to anyone. He left his past in the past and continued to serve a God who had a plan for him, and guess what? He has a plan for each of us. I, too, have many things in my past I am not proud of. Maybe some of you have also done things that you kicked yourself for doing. Just remember God forgave David, He never left him, and He continued to bless him and use him until he died. He will do the same for you. Just ask him. Then go ahead and read the story of David for yourself. It will be well worth your time.

****

Do Not Fear

If you haven't heard of the coronavirus, you must be under 2 years of age. The news of its effects is widely being shouted from small towns to large cities. Get prepared. Don't shake hands, don't hug, wash your hands, wash your hands, wash your hands is the chant we hear everywhere. Stay away from large crowds, don't go on vacation, make sure you have food in your cupboard, and of course, toilet paper in your bathroom. This virus, like all other viruses, is unseen to the naked eye. They lay around on counter tops, in bathrooms, on grocery carts and they attach themselves to us as we are going about our daily lives. Then we get sick. Then lots of people get sick, and we reach a point of mass hysteria where no one wants to go outside of their homes. I get it, we need to be cautious and mindful of others, but I am choosing not to live in the fear of the mass hysteria, because I too know of Someone unseen. Someone who has more power than any germ on a countertop. He brings order to chaos, He brings peace to the stressed, He brings hope to the hurting, and He has told me over and over in His word...DO NOT FEAR! I am throwing all my cares on the unseen, and you can, too...HIS name is Jesus.

****

"Mary Did You Know" is probably one of my favorite Christmas carols.

It asks the question several times, Mary, did you know that your baby boy would one day...and I wonder, did she know? Did she know her baby boy would walk on water? Did she know that her baby boy would save her sons and daughters? Did she know the child she held in her arms was the Lord of all creation? I think any mom can identify with this song. We can all remember holding our children and peering into their innocent faces as we wondered what we did to deserve this priceless gift we held in our arms. Mary was like us. Except, she peered into the face of God, a gift not only to her, but to the whole world. She looked into the face of her Savior, and her child. So the question of "Mary, did you know?" is one that I would like to ask too. She knew from the beginning that her baby was special but did she know who He was? Did she know at that moment the sacrifice He would make for the whole world? A sacrifice that would bring any mother to the depths of agony and dark sorrow. I am not privy to what Mary knew or what she didn't know about her child. What she did know was that she held Love in her arms that day. And I am thankful for her, a young girl, who said yes to God. And one day, I will be able to ask Mary this question face to face..."Mary Did You Know." Why not take a listen to the song today.

****

Do you see what I see? Do you hear what I hear?

As the song continues, it asks other questions all pointing to the birth of Jesus. Looking around today, I ask myself what do I see? I see anger, I see hopelessness, I see frustration, I see loss of jobs, I see sickness, and I see family discourse, just to name a few. Then I am reminded that I must not see this world through earthly eyes. I must put on spiritual glasses and then focus on the world around me. Oh, and if I look intently, I can see kindness, I can see hope, I can see goodness, and mercy, and thankfully I can still see joy. All of these things are there right along with hopelessness and despair. I must look deeply for them. Then I ask myself...what am I hearing? I hear fighting, and grieving, I hear crying, and pain, I hear the groaning of a world that is spinning out of control. I am again reminded that I need to listen to the small voice inside of me, and when I listen to Jesus, I start to hear what is often being hidden underneath the chaos. If I listen I can hear joy. I can hear it in a baby's laughter; I can hear it in the ringing of a bell outside of a store. I can hear it as kind words are spoken, I can hear it when love screams louder than hate. So this year, the lesson for me is that I must put on the filter that lets me see and hear this world through Jesus, for when I do, it is only then that I can truly see and hear the sounds of love in action. Just as it was when He appeared in a manger so long ago. What glasses and hearing aids are you using today?

****

I bring you tidings of great joy!

It is a time for joy. The angel proclaimed it..."Do not fear....I bring you good tidings of great joy!" Jesus is the joy at Christmas and throughout the year. Joy and the year 2020 seem to have little in common. That would be true if joy was temporary and fleeting. But true joy comes from within. It comes from knowing that in all circumstances, when life is out of control, when I can't see any way out of a problem, when I am filled with grief; even then I know where my joy comes from. It cannot be shaken by something on the outside because it lives on the inside. It lives in the knowledge that Jesus came to us as a Savior, a King, a baby in a manger and He has called us not to fear and has brought us joy. When Jesus has made His home in your heart, the joy is always there. Like the song says: I've got the joy, joy, joy, joy down in my heart. Where? Down in my heart to stay. Praying that your Christmas will be filled with His joy.

Check out the Christmas story in Luke 2.

****

Christmas 2020 is over.

Yesterday while many of you were enjoying your family gathering, ours was quiet. I knew that we would celebrate a day later than most. And now ours is over too. We prepare for this day for so long, we look for that perfect gift for our loved ones, we wrap gifts till our fingers and back ache, and then we consume such yummy food that we tend to keep it with us months after the holidays are over. I guess you could say that about sums up my last few weeks. Yesterday though, as you were celebrating, I couldn't stop thinking about a family whose father was in the hospital and very close to dying. What was their Christmas like? I also thought about a family whose father passed away just a few days before Christmas, and I wondered would there be any joy in their house? It seems in this life we walk hand in hand with joy and sadness. None of us get past it. I remember a time in my life when everything stopped because of a trial I was going through. I couldn't believe the whole world didn't stop too, but it just continued on. So today, even in my joy of having my family all together, (the first time in 7 years) my heart is breaking for families that are in pain. They will look at the Christmas of 2020 with sadness and pain. So as we share our joys, I pray that we are always mindful of those whose joy is being hidden under a blanket of tears. I do believe that when Jesus said your mourning will turn to joy, He knew what He was talking about. Trust Him.

****

Who Do You Say I Am?

This morning I was reading in the Gospel of Luke, and Jesus asked his disciples, "Who do you say that I am?" Many years ago I helped put together a musical for some of the teens at The Cornerstone Youth Center. It was titled "The Witness." Maybe some of you remember it; maybe some of you were in it. There is a part in the musical where Jesus asks Peter that very same question. "Who do you say that I am?" Immediately after the question is asked, Peter sings a song that responds to that question. "You are the Christ, the Son of the Living God, I say you are the Christ...You are my Lord." Isn't it strange how some songs stay with you? Well, every time I hear that question asked, whether in a sermon, or my own reading, or a message on the radio, my spirit starts to sing that refrain. I often wonder if my mind and heart are just as engaged. Do I really believe what my spirit so easily sings? I have not liked this stay at home order, but it has certainly brought to light many areas of my life that need to be reminded who Jesus is: He is the Christ, Lord of my life. That same Jesus continues to ask each of us the same question. "Who do you say that I am?" Don't ignore the question. Your answer will have eternal consequences.

****

The First Miracle

Mother's Day is fast approaching. Reading in John chapter 2, I realized that Jesus had a soft spot for his mom. The setting was the wedding in Cana. If you are at all familiar with Jesus and His teachings, you know this is where He performed His first public miracle. I have read this story many times and yet today the Spirit spoke to me in a couple different ways. First, Jesus' mother was aware of the host having run out of wine, which was a serious thing to happen in those days. It wasn't her wedding, so why did she care? But she did, and she went to her son and shared this dilemma with him. His reply, "My time has not yet come." Mary didn't respond to Jesus, but she left the wine problem in His hands. Did she know that He would take care of it? What was going through Jesus' mind? He knew it wasn't His time, but He loved His mother. I think He would have done just about anything to help her, and she felt bad for the hosts of this wedding. She looked at the servants and said, "Do whatever he tells you." That's it. Listen to Jesus. Do what He says. Mary already knew that whatever Jesus would do, it would be the right thing. In life today, isn't that all we need to know too?

Jesus, knowing it was not His time yet but loving his mother, spoke to the servants. He commanded them to "Fill the jars with water." Water? Isn't it wine that was needed? I am sure at this time I might have been tempted to explain that to Jesus, but they never hesitated. They filled the jars to the brim with water. Then He told them, "Now draw some out and take it to the master of the banquet." And they did! When the servants dipped into the jar to serve to the host, it was water. Were they scared to give it the host? It was water!!! Just when did it become wine? Was it on the way to the master of the banquet? Was it when it touched the banquet master's lips? And when did the servants know? The text does not tell us when the water miraculously changed into wine, only that it did. I can only

108

imagine the servants' awe at what had just happened: they served up water...and Jesus produced fine wine.

The end of the story, you can already guess. Everyone was thrilled with the wine. The servants knew without a doubt who was responsible for this miracle. And I like to think that maybe, just maybe, this is where the real Mother's Day started. The love in action of a son loving His mother. Take a minute to read John 2:1-11.

****

Children Sermon time again.

It's funny how these pop into my mind and make a home there until I write them down, so here we go. A few years ago we were heading to Hawaii. Hawaii is beautiful and I loved being there, but the plane trip seemed to take forever. After we had boarded our plane, listened to the flight attendant, fastened our seat belts, we were good to go. Only a few more hours and we would be there. It was one of those days that the clouds were above us, below us and completely surrounding us. They were not foggy but instead were beautiful white billowy clouds. This was a smooth ride. Several hours had passed and I heard a voice over the loudspeaker to get our seatbelt on as were going to prepare for landing. I looked out the window and saw nothing that even resembled land anywhere. And yet, this pilot was telling us to prepare. He reminded us a few times. Get our seatbelt on (mine never came off), put our things under the seat, it's time to land. Then I felt the plane as it started to descend. It was going down. I still only saw clouds. I had no control and if I did, I would still to this day be lost in the clouds somewhere. I was totally in the pilot's hands. I sat back, took a deep breath and waited. Just before our landing we broke through the clouds and we were lined up with a runway directly in front of us. I let out the air that had been building in my chest and what I saw out the window was the paradise I was waiting for. We were safe. I learned a few lessons in life from that descent. 1. Make sure you choose and listen to the right pilot. (Jesus) 2. Even when I can't see my way out, my Pilot knows the way. (Trust) 3. Do what the Pilot says. (Obey) You will get to paradise; choose your pilot wisely.

****

Hypocrite

Writing has become therapeutic for me. It lets me toss things around in my head for a few days, and then I sit down and try to make sense of it in writing. Since our Sunday Sermon I have been mulling over in my mind the subject of the sermon. It was "hypocrite!" Yup, how dare our Pastor talk about hypocrites in church? I was well aware of the fact that even before he started this sermon, I would identify with it. (I don't think I was alone) A hypocrite says one thing but does another. Oh, I have been there many times. It is something that I have tried to conquer, but in my own strength it just doesn't happen. I have heard it said many times that the church is full of hypocrites, and I have to believe it is true. As well as your grocery stores, your ball games, your bars...it is obvious to me that everywhere people are, you will find hypocrites. And I will be among them. As Jesus followers we are called to be different from the world, and we as Christians try to live a life that gives glory to God, and yet we are constantly continuing to fail. Yes, I am a Christian, and all of you that know me already know that I am not perfect. But thankfully, I know One who is. In this world of craziness God sent His son, Jesus to pay for my sins, because He knew we could never reach perfection. So, today, I will thank God that even in my hypocritical times, and my outright sin, the price for it has been paid. With forgiveness given and accepted, I can start again. So, when you hear others say the Church is full of hypocrites, agree with them, for we know we are not perfect, and we never will be on this earth. Thanks Pastor Mike McCrumb for your series on "Little Sins". I am certainly identifying with them. And I am reminded each week that we really are all a work in progress.

****

Blessings

Aren't we all a bit on the edge these days? Seems like it doesn't take much to get me frustrated and I am usually pretty easy going. Yesterday a friend shared with me his frustration in buying a washing machine, last night my mom was frustrated with her cell phone that seemed to be stuck, and this morning I drove to Plainwell to do some banking, and for some reason not shared with their patrons, it was closed! I found myself feeling that gnawing anger starting to build as I pulled out of the parking lot and headed for the

Richland branch. It was then I looked at my watch and smiled. Yesterday at a garage sale (of course) I bought a watch that made me smile when I saw it, and it has made me smile each time I look at it. A one dollar investment that has already earned a great return for me. In all my frustrations and all the chaos of the world around us, God uniquely placed a cast off from someone else to bring me joy. In the book of James, it tells us that "Every good and perfect gift is from above." Today as I wear my new watch, I am reminded that all we have to do is look for the gifts He has given us. They even might be hiding at the next garage sale.

****

Depression

There is something about this writing thing that I don't really understand. I call it the writing urge. Not that it happens every day, not that it even happens every week, but when it does happen, I have to sit down and let my heart show up on the blank screen before me. Today is like that. I must fill this blank screen in front of me with words that I hope will make sense to you as well as myself. So, today I write. I have never really dealt with depression as some of you have. Oh, I have down days; don't we all? But the type of depression that is always lurking around the corner waiting to smother you is not my reality. Even though it is not my reality, I know it is very real for some. It is a darkness that some face every day. I am not dealing with any health issues today, but many of my family and friends live with pain and illness with each passing day. I know their struggle is real. Today, I have food, today I have a house to live in, today I have the love of my family, today I must enjoy all that I have, because all I have is today. I am not guaranteed tomorrow, nor do I know what tomorrow will bring to me. Tomorrow might bring sickness, tomorrow might bring pain of loss, tomorrow might not come. I must stop in the midst of the madness of this world today and recognize the joy that today brings. It is in savoring the joy of the moment today that will make the trials of tomorrow fade a bit. I must live my best today, in whatever situation I am in, for as the saying goes, "Don't worry about tomorrow...God is already there." I pray that each of us will go and enjoy TODAY!

****

Children's Sermon

I did a children's sermon a few years ago that included 4 of my grandchildren. I called all of them up front to join me, then I turned them around so they could not see the congregation. I explained to them that when they heard their dad's voice they were to turn around. Of course, I had several men in the congregation say to them, "Norris kids, turn around." Not once were my grandchildren ever tempted to turn around at the voices from the other men. Then at last I had their dad ask them to turn around, and do you know what? At the first word out of their dad's mouth, each one of my grandkids turned immediately. No hesitations, no wondering if it really was his voice. They knew it. They lived with that voice; there was absolutely no doubt in their mind. It was the voice of the man who loved them. I am sure you are wondering why I am telling you this story. For the last few weeks, I have been listening to and allowing the voices on Facebook and the media to invade my mind. In the midst of it, I found myself frustrated beyond belief, uncertain of the world around me, and just plain wore out. I needed to shut out what everyone else was saying and listen to what God was saying. He is still speaking to us, you know. Do you know His voice when He speaks? Can you hear it above the shouting voices of this world? His voice brings calm, His voice brings hope, and His voice brings peace, not as the world gives...for He says in John 16:33 "In this world you will have trouble...take heart I have overcome the world." It just doesn't get any better than that. I choose to stop listening to what the world tells me...for it can never bring the peace that God gives.

****

Church in the midst of Covid

Today we were able to meet inside of our church building. We have been looking forward to it for at least 10 weeks, and it was good to be back. But it was different. I should not have been surprised; hasn't all life been different lately? Our church usually has a teaching time before the service; you might remember calling it Sunday School. I love sitting with a group of adults as we discuss the Scripture of the day or whatever might be on our hearts from the previous week. It just doesn't get any better than to have a cup of coffee and share a snack as we share our lives and the love of Jesus with each other. That was not an option today. Only the Sunday worship service. The people who attend our church, well, I have always considered them my extended family. It was exciting to watch them come inside today for the service, instead of staying in our cars in the parking lot. But it was different. There were smiles but no hugs. Did you know that when you look at someone's eyes, even as a mask covers their nose and mouth, you can tell they are smiling? It was great to see, but different. There were many seats to sit in, but you couldn't be close to anyone. Good to be inside, but it was different. We all wanted to be there, we are family, but it was different. As Pastor Mike McCrumb started his sermon which happened to be on the sin of anger, I realized that I was angry at not being able to do church as usual. It has all changed. And I really don't like it. As usual when I get angry, I let it simmer for a while and then hopefully deal with it without losing my cool. It doesn't happen all the time, but today as I am dealing with this anger of change, I can almost hear God speak to me as He says, "Everything else might change, but not Me. I am the same, yesterday, today, and forever." That is what I needed to be reminded of today. My God is faithful, unchanging, and thankfully loaded with patience!

****

Truth

I am trying to make some sense of life as we know it now, and for some reason nothing makes sense anymore. Oh common sense where have you gone? I am pretty sure at this point in our lives we are all realizing that life will never be "like it used to be" ever again. Will we forever see signs on doors that require masks for entering? Will our time of hugs and laughter and closeness ever return? Will we ever see our children play sports for fun? What will our schools look like? Will my granddaughter finally have a graduation ceremony? Will our hatred toward each other stop rearing its ugly head? I see this manifested on Facebook every day. It is in the political posts as well as the "for your own good" posts. It is in the sarcasm and slants we all want to put on our way of thinking. Because we know each of us is right, and of course the other person is wrong. I am a nobody in the big scheme of things; my opinions are just that...opinions. I will never be able to argue you into believing the way I feel, nor will you be able to convince me into believing your way. We each have been influenced by life, and we see things

113

differently. My opinion, your opinion doesn't really matter. Truth is what matters. It can't be your truth and my truth because they are probably different. Truth is absolute. It is the age-old question we all must ask, "What is Truth?" I find my answer in what Jesus said. "I am the Way, the Truth and the Life." When I focus on His Truth, all the opinions, all the fighting, all the sadness and hopelessness fade into the darkness as the Light of His Truth is allowed to shine in my world.

Hoping we can someday all agree on Truth.

****

Prayer

There are times that I pray on paper. Not for anyone else to see, just a plea from my heart to God. I happened to read one of the prayers that I had written on January 2nd this year. It struck me that with all that has gone on this year I should share this with you. My heart. "Christmas 2019 has passed and the New Year is looking me right in the face. What will You bring to my life this year? I am pretty sure I will be met with joy, sadness, doubting and a bit of wonder. You know, you wonder if you will get through another day. You wonder if life will ever be normal again. And I wonder in the knowledge of YOU. You, my Savior, control my days. You walk with me in the dark days as well as the joyous times. There is not one breath I will breathe without You filling me with Your Spirit. Oh, how can I fear anything? You are everywhere; You are my God, my Savior, my Deliverer, and my Comforter...In YOU will I find rest in 2020." Who knew what the next few months would bring? Glad I had the foresight to know Who is in control.

****

Offering

It is a word that our culture often makes sound like churches just want your money. I do get it, and some churches might sound like that. For the past few weeks, the story in the Bible of the widow that gave all she had to the temple treasury has been crossing my mind. So today I decided to re-read the story. For the most part since I became a Christian I have tithed. Not because I thought I was better for doing it, but because I have always felt called to give back.

I began to wonder about myself today as I re-read the story in Luke 21. The setting takes place at a place of worship. In today's terms, the plate was being passed. And Jesus was watching. He doesn't make a negative comment about those who were rich and gave. But He does see this poor widow drop in 2 coins. It was all she had. She didn't have a 401K; she didn't have a savings account, she had 2 coins. And she gave them to God. That is when I started to wonder about me. Has my giving become so routine that it really doesn't cost me anything? She gave all she had, and trusted God for everything else. Wow. I, like the others that gave that day, often give out of my wealth, and not with all I have. I don't think for one minute that God is telling us to give all we have, but this widow gave from her heart. I think that is what I am supposed to realize today.

My giving needs to have my heart in it, my act of worship to God who has given me so much. No matter how much it is. Giving gets us outside of who we are and reminds us that it is not all about us. Thank you, Jesus, for Your gentle reminder to me.

****

Embraced

A little boy with cancer was asked by his doctor who he would like to meet. His response: "Batman." The video clip was touching as the doctor had Batman walk the hall to be introduced to this very sick little boy. As the little boy approached Batman, he opened his cape and invited him in for a big, long and tender hug! You have probably seen the clip too, but this morning when I watched it, I couldn't help but think that this is what it will be like when we see Jesus. As I watched that little boy snuggle in for a hug and a hand reach up to bring his head in for a complete cover, the boy melted into his chest. Oh, how we long for that as Christians, being in the arms of Jesus where nothing can hurt us, all cares of this life are gone and the only thing we are surrounded with is total love in His arms.

****

This World is not my Home

Am I the only one that is having trouble even turning on the news anymore? I used to be a news junkie. I loved watching it,

115

listening to it, reading it, you name it... I loved the news. Not anymore. I am just sad about what is going on in our world. Just when did we decide it was okay to watch as our history was being torn down before our eyes? When did we give the okay to loot and destroy and call it peaceful protest? When did we decide it was time to throw out our police force to get rid of it all because of a few bad ones? I will never understand this way of thinking. There is a verse in the Bible that speaks of Jesus as He looks over the city of Jerusalem and He says, "How often have I longed to gather your children together, as a hen gathers her chicks under her wings, but you were not willing. Look, your house is desolate." My mind keeps going over this verse as I see our country in total chaos. Our country has gone from a place of freedom to a land held captive. It is heartbreaking and beyond understanding. Thankfully, my peace comes not from this world, because there is no peace here. My security lies not in anything this world offers because it can be lost in a minute, and my joy does not come from the things of this earth because it is not lasting. My home is not here, I'm just passing through. Thankfully, it is knowing Jesus that brings me real peace, true security, and overflowing joy. I hope the same for you.

****

Adoption

Several years ago, our family was blessed with an adoption of a grandson from Ethiopia. I remember the first pictures of him that were sent to his anxiously awaiting parents. Who says they don't believe in love at first sight? Our whole family fell in love with this little boy in the picture. We waited many months before he was able to join our family and by then he was already a part of us. I can still picture this beautiful baby boy with the biggest, brightest eyes and even bigger smile as his mom carried him towards us in the airport. You are probably wondering why I am sharing this story with you today. Watching the news recently has stirred feelings within me about my grandson who just happens to have darker skin than us. Will he be safe? Will he be hated because his skin is different? What will his world look like? How will you look at him? We must search our hearts and find love for each other and not hate. Just look at us. We all come in different sizes, colors and shapes. Yet we are all made in the image of God. I want to close my eyes to the hate around us; I want to shout to the world that who we are goes so much deeper than our skin color. But, really, don't we already know that? So, I ask you...will you pray for a better world for all our children and grandchildren? They deserve it. It must start with us!

****

Another Mother's Day

Tomorrow is Mother's Day, and I am beyond thankful that my mom is still with us at 90 years old. Wishing her a Happy Mother's Day, even if it is over the phone, will bring joy. But today as I was looking for a photo, I came across this one. Yes, it is me, along with the two boys that gave me the name "Mom". What do you know about raising kids at the age of 17? For that matter what do you know about it at any age? And yet, as moms we are given this awesome responsibility of raising our children without a "How To" manual. At times we think we do everything wrong, and other times we think we rock at parenting, and somehow in the mix of all our best efforts, God steps in. He stepped in many times during the years that I was trying my best to parent. There are no "do overs" in parenting. It is a one-shot deal. That is where faith comes in. I guess what I really wanted to say is Thank you to my sons for making me a mom. The way you live your lives is a testimony to God's faithfulness in the life of a 17-year-old girl.

****

More Holy Week thoughts

Today is Palm Sunday, and I have had this picture burned in my mind since our service this morning.

Okay, most of us know that on Palm Sunday the palm branches are handed out and there is a parade of children and some brave adults that wave their branches while singing, "Hosanna" around the church. This is a great reminder of the crowd that greeted Jesus as He rode into Jerusalem. Our Pastor Mike McCrumb also spoke of the coats that the crowd laid down for Jesus. He explained to us that people's outer garments back in that day told who they were. It was their identity, and they were laying their identity down to be counted for Christ. It was then that our Pastor removed his coat and laid it on the floor. He was showing us that he has laid down his identity for Christ. It was looking at his coat on the floor in front of the altar that burns in my mind. Many in the crowd on that first Palm Sunday laid their coats down for Jesus. They were all in on that day, but we know what Friday brings. Some of them picked their coats back up, or dragged it along with them as they yelled, "Crucify Him!" Today as I and others laid their coats on the floor at the altar in a small act of showing we were giving up our identity for Christ's, I am praying that I wouldn't be found in the group denying Christ, but I know I am not much different from the people in that crowd. What about you? That He still chose to die for us is a love beyond understanding.

****

Judas. I don't know why he is on my mind today. Probably because tomorrow will be the day that changed his life forever. Every Easter season his name is there. Most everyone has heard of Judas. The friend no one wants to have in your circle. He betrayed Jesus for 30 pieces of silver. He lived with Jesus for three years, learned from him, saw his miracles and I just have to think he loved him too. Yet, he went to the chief priest and conspired to turn Jesus in. Betrayal done. Then he went back and had supper with him. And Jesus let him. He even washed his feet. The King, bending to wash the feet of a man who is set on betrayal. A betrayal that would begin a series of events that changed the world. A betrayal that would give the name of Judas a black spot in history for all time. A betrayal that as much as I am disgusted with, I can say I identify with. How many times have I betrayed Christ? More times than I want to acknowledge. And thankfully that same Jesus who bent to wash the feet of his betrayer, knowing what was to come, still chose to hang on a cross and die. And the blood He shed upon that cross continues to drip from Calvary to me and you. Soon it will be Friday but praise God, Sunday is coming!

****

Each year during Holy Week, I try to read the Gospel account of the events that led up to the Crucifixion and Resurrection. It seems each year that different things stand out to me. Trying to understand the "why" in so many areas of Jesus' trial and His beating stood out to me this year. Why did everyone taunt Him, make fun of Him and mock Him? I just don't get it. He was not speaking back to them, He was silent. He was not fighting back. He was the receiver of hate, pain and rejection for doing nothing wrong. I realize in order to inflict pain on others intentionally you have to minimize their worth; you have to place yourself on a higher level and of more value than the one being hurt. And that is what they did. They beat Him, laughed at Him, and taunted Him, then led Him off to die. But why? He is the only One that could look past their hurling insults, look past their laughter in His pain, look past their hatred and still go to His death for them. Who does that? And why? I will never understand the suffering, I will never understand the rejection, and I will never understand that He did it all because of His Love for us! I won't understand it, but I will always be in awe that He died for me. Salvation is free for all of us, but it was not cheap. Why not read it for yourself.

****

It is part of His plan. It always has been from that very first sin. Today, the sacrifice is set. Today is Good Friday. Was it good on that day so long ago? Would I have called it good if I had to watch a crucifixion? Not just any crucifixion, but one where my loved one was beyond recognition, withering in pain and agony nailed to a cross? I try to put myself at the foot of the cross that day. I would have heard him say, "Forgive them, for they know not what they do." and I am sure I would wonder how He could forgive. I would have heard Him say, "My God, My God, why have you forsaken me?" And I would have wondered where God was at that moment. I would have heard Him say, "It is finished." What is finished? He's dead. I am sure I would have been relieved at the moment that His suffering was over, and I would have pondered in my heart if what He said was true. Was He the Messiah? I think I would have cried until there were no more tears left in me. Jesus... dead. Today, there is nothing good about it; they killed my Savior. But, it is still Friday and He tells me to wait...Sunday is coming...you will see!

****

If I had just watched Jesus die on the cross, what would I have done the next day? Saturday. I know I would relive the event over and over in my mind: His agony and suffering, then His final last breath. How could I get my mind to even think He would rise again? I saw Him die. So, it's Saturday, and I am in a mixture of doubt and faith. What was it He told us? He would rise after three days? I am just not sure now...I saw Him die. How will that be possible? And yet, there it is in my heart, a trust, a belief, a peace I don't understand. How can this be? The man who said He was the Messiah, who we loved and followed. Today is Saturday and He is dead. My grief is overwhelming, but there it is, hiding behind my doubt: HOPE. It is Saturday, but Sunday is coming!

****

The tomb is empty. Oh, for us it brings great joy. To those that arrived at the tomb that morning to see the stone rolled away, an empty tomb meant confusion, sadness and overwhelming loss.

Who would take the body of their Lord? I love John's telling of the empty tomb story. Mary Magdalene arrives at the tomb first, and she alerts the disciples, who run to the tomb to find it empty.

No one understood what was going on. They only knew the body was gone. Now what? They all left and went back home. All except Mary Magdalene. She lingered at the tomb. She stayed, and Jesus showed up. Oh, she thought He was the gardener, and when He asked why she was crying, and who she was looking for, she responded with, "Did you take the body?" Did Jesus look different? Why didn't she recognize him? Have you ever been in a situation where you are talking to someone, but you really don't see them? A drive-through bank teller comes to my mind. I think that is what was happening to Mary. She was so grieved that she didn't recognize who she was talking to. Her mind was going in a hundred different directions until He spoke her name. "Mary." That is all it took. She recognized his voice. She knew it was Him. He is Risen! Don't let this day go by without hearing Jesus call your name. In her deepest grief and sorrow she heard Him call her name and her world was never the same again. He is Risen. He is Risen, indeed.

****

His Perfect Time

There is a verse in the Bible found in Galatians and this morning it has come across my feed from two different people. It is a familiar verse to me. As a matter of fact, when I had coffee mugs made for the Center a few years ago, it was the verse I used on them.

It says, "Let us not grow weary in doing good, for at the proper time we will reap a harvest if we do not give up." It is an encouragement to press on, to keep up the work of doing good, and when nothing seems to be going right, press on. Sometimes I want to scream at God and say just when is the proper time? I am growing weary here. His response: Don't give up. I see you. I know what you're going through. I will not be late or early when it comes to the proper time. Trust me, my timing is perfect.

Read it for yourself...Galatians 6:9.

****

Speechless!

This does not describe who I am normally. But today, I am left speechless as I read a post from a nurse who is doing her job tending to those who have this virus. My mind cannot comprehend what they are facing at this moment as they watch people slowly die and feeling so helpless. It gives me a wakeup call, and leaves me speechless. Where do empathy and selfishness ever meet? They don't. I cannot be selfish and love others too. I have to become less important for others to become the most important. Those working in the medical field today have my utmost respect, for they are living their lives full of empathy, compassion, and love. Those qualities are revealed to us when we are tested. I complain, and they step up to the plate. I must learn over and over again that it is not about me; it never has been. This week is Holy Week, and I am reminded again that Jesus laid down His life for me, selfish person that I am. Help me, Lord, to see the needs of others, and help me to get out of the way so You can work through me. Today I am speechless, but thanks to Jesus I am not hopeless.

****

Blindness

I am approaching the 66th year in my life and I am pretty sure I have never prayed to be blind. But I think that is exactly what many of us need to be praying for. If we could just take our masks and pull them up over our eyes as well, maybe, just maybe, we would see some real changes in our world. Color would disappear, and the ability to read signs and Facebook posts would be much harder.

Maybe we would even begin to like each other again, in spite of who we vote for. I have this picture in my mind that I am walking on a very narrow pier, and in the water on both sides are friends of mine. They are in no danger of drowning, but they all want me in on their side of the water. They are each giving me thoughtful reasons why I should join them. Some are quiet, some yell at me and a few are downright obnoxious. I know I can't join either side; I have to do what is right for me. So I walk, trying to avoid getting pulled into the water, but they won't let up and they continue to grab at my feet. If I get too close they will pull me in. When I focus on not getting pulled in the water, I actually lose my balance and start slipping. It is only when I look ahead to the end of the pier and see who is guiding my steps and encouraging me to not look on either side that I find my strength to stay out of the water. Jesus is there beckoning me straight toward Him. When my eyes connect with His, the walk is no longer a struggle. I stay on dry ground and have no fear of falling. In this hate-filled world today, my prayer is to be blind to the things that would pull me away from Jesus, and to be able to stay on the path He has called me to. Maybe a little blindness could help all of us.

****

No Writing in the Sky

Last week I was spending time at our cottage, trying to find some direction in a decision with which I was struggling. It was a quiet place, a place where I could shut out the world and seek direction from God. It was a great time of reflection. But God remained silent. Ever had that happen? Oh, I was hoping for writing in the sky, or maybe another talking animal, but nope, just silence. I could get all worried that God didn't hear my pleas, or that He doesn't really care about my small decisions, but in reality what I learned was and it has always been true, no matter what choice I make, He walks beside me, He goes before me and quite often He pushes me from behind. He never leaves me. Slowly in His time, not mine, He will reveal to me what I need to do. For now, I will thank Him for the gift of a much-needed time out!

****

Let your Light Shine

This little light of mine, I'm gonna let it shine! Do you remember that song? We still sing it every once in a while in church. Interesting isn't it, that to let our light shine the most, it needs to be in a dark place. I have listened and cried with hurting women for a long time now, hearing heartbreaking stories of drug abuse, physical and sexual abuse that never leave you. Trying to remain strong as you listen, when what you really want to do is break down and cry and cover your ears to block out what you are hearing. You wish you were as far removed from this situation as you can get. To know the evil that exists in this world and to see the brokenness it brings is sometimes too much. And yet, I am called to shine His Light where He has placed me. So tonight, as I sing the rest of the song, "Let it shine, let it shine, let it shine," I am praying for strength to keep the light flickering, because shining tonight is hard.

****

Lent

Today is the first day of Lent. Often in churches it begins with a pastor marking a cross on your forehead with ashes. Some churches participate, some don't. I remember the first time I noticed this sight. It was on a couple of women at a restaurant. I had no clue why they had what looked like black smudges on their foreheads. What I really wanted to do was to get their attention and tell them they had a spot of dirt on their head. I was sure they probably didn't know it was there. We have all been there. If you have extra food on your face and someone kindly tells you to wipe it off. That is what I wanted to do. I am not sure about the origins of the mark, but since that day in the restaurant I have learned a bit more about the ashes. I have in fact taken part in an ashes service at the beginning of Lent. During this time of year, the 40 days before Easter (Lent) is a time that we as Christians prepare our minds and hearts for the coming days ahead. Some people give up something they enjoy during this time, like dessert, coffee, television, etc. I am not sure where that came from either. What I do know is for Christians it is an important time of the year. Just as the days leading up to Christmas (Advent) bring us joy, the days leading up to Easter bring us joy too. We remember. We remember the sacrifice on a cross, we remember the love that was shown, and we remember the victory over death at the resurrection. Sound a bit strange to you? Why not take some time during these 40 days of Lent to get to know more about Jesus? Go check out a church in your area. Why not tag along with a friend. Every church I know is filled with people who started out wondering what this Jesus is all about. Why not you?

****

The love of the Father

A few years ago I shared a children's sermon in church, and for some reason it keeps going through my mind, so today it is in yours too. The story begins at a girls' softball game. It was my granddaughter's game, and she was in the 3rd or 4th grade. It was her turn to bat. Of course, as a grandma I was watching intently the scene before me. The ball was pitched, the ball was hit, and she proceeded to run to first base. There was a collision with the first baseman and Abby went down. She popped up pretty quick, and was called out, but we could tell she was hurting. Nothing serious, but she was in pain and was trying to hold back the tears as she exited the field. It was then I noticed her eyes find her dad, and she made a line straight to him. Not looking around, only straight ahead to where her dad was. Their eyes locked. When she got closer to him, I could see a tear release and a hurting young girl drop in to the lap of her father. I couldn't look away. She was in the arms of her dad. She was being held with a love that they both shared. A father and a daughter. It wasn't too long before Abby was calm and ready to go back to the game. Her father gently lifted her off his lap and set her on her way. She had a game to finish. I pondered that scene that is still so vivid in my mind today, knowing that I had just witnessed what our Heavenly Father does for His children. When we hurt, we run to Him. We climb into His lap, we get comforted, we get calmed, and we hear Him whisper, "It's time to go out and finish the game." Are you in the process of being hurt? Run to Him. Are you in His lap? Enjoy His comfort. Or are you getting ready to finish the game? Whatever place you find yourself, He is there!

****

Garage Sales, Christmas and the lost baby Jesus

If you know me well, you know that I love garage sales. At any given sale you can find Christmas decorations of all kinds. It seems we are a country obsessed with snowmen, Santa, reindeer and angels, and we change them often. That's why we find them at every sale. I like browsing the

Christmas stuff, but I am drawn to nativity sets. The more unique they are, the more I like them. A few years ago, I found one that looked like a clay Mexican set, unique for sure, and of course I bought it. As the lady wrapped each piece individually for me, we talked about how cool the set was. And I left with a smile. Christmas was obviously a few months away, so I put it with my Christmas stuff and forgot about it until December. I brought it out with the other sets I have and I started unwrapping each piece, setting them out as I admired the detail on each one. I had it all: Wise men, shepherds, animals, Mary and Joseph and angels. It was all there-except for Jesus. I searched the wrapping, I dug through the box and I still couldn't find Jesus. I am sure I left him at the sale. In my conversation with the woman wrapping the other pieces, I didn't make sure I had the whole set. Jesus got left behind. I had an incomplete set. I decided to set it out anyway, and you know what? This set has now become my favorite nativity set. You see, it is a reminder to me not to get caught up in the trappings of what the world says Christmas is, because when I do, I forget Jesus. It is my reminder that I can have everything else that goes with the nativity, but if I don't have Jesus, then nothing is complete.

****

Christmas

Today a song that came out a few years ago has been running through my mind. I have no idea who wrote it, or who sang it, but I can't shake the words. "Where's the line to see Jesus?" Six words, but they have made me stop and listen to that still small voice. We have our kids wait in line to sit on Santa's lap, we get in line and wait to drive through a Christmas light display, we wait in line to buy presents, but have I stopped even once this season to get a look at Jesus?

We all know there is no line to get in at the mall to see Him, so where do you see Him? I realized that I saw Him yesterday as I visited with a friend in a nursing home, I saw Him Friday in the faces of my grandkids as we made cookies, and I saw Him today in church.

He was there as our kids learned about His birth and the events that surrounded it, He was sitting with a friend who is going through her first Christmas without her dad, He was holding a friend who couldn't stop the tears from running down her face from family difficulties, and He was helping a friend as she struggled to breathe with her oxygen tank in tow. A kind word spoken, a hug shared, acts of kindness given...you see, you can see Jesus when you see others with HIS eyes. So, who will you see as you wait in line to see Jesus? Look around, you don't want to miss Him.

****

God with Us

It's the day after Christmas. The hustle and bustle of getting everything ready is over. The cards I meant to send are still in the box from the store, and the dirty dishes from a yummy dinner are looking at me from the sink. I can see remnants of wrapping paper peeking at me from under the couch as the smell of a new candle is filling my home. It's the day after Christmas. And I am reflecting. Christmas. "God with us," It is easy to say, but this year it was what we held on to.

After enjoying a great Christmas dinner with family and friends, we set out to open gifts! It doesn't matter what age you are, most of us like gifts. I love giving them, and yes, I love to see what is inside a box wrapped for me too. I guess the kid in me will never grow old.

Almost as soon as we finished eating, Val (my son's girlfriend) got a call that her daughter (Olivia) was being taken to the hospital. She had started to bleed; gushing is the word I remember them saying, from having her tonsils removed a few days before. "God with us." We stopped and prayed before Val left our house for the drive to the hospital. Not knowing what she would find when she arrived, we wanted her to know that God is with her. Surgery would be needed to stop the bleeding, on Christmas day. Thankfully, there was a surgeon who was away from his family to take care of the needs of our family. "God with us." The surgery took place quickly. It was over and successful. "God with us." She was back in her room, I am sure a bit scared and pretty tired, right along with a mom who was drained. To their surprise they were greeted with a box of gifts.

Who would think about gifts for someone in the hospital on Christmas day? Of course, it would be a family that had spent hours with their sick daughter at the hospital. They were giving to someone they would never meet. They would never see the joy on the face of the one receiving the gift, but they gave. "God with us."

Liv will be coming home today. And we have learned that "God with us" came as a baby in a manger over 2,000 years ago, yet He is with us at this very moment. I hope each of you will remember that "God with us" has come for all of us...not just on Christmas, but every day.

****

The Returned Christmas Card

A few days ago, a Christmas card that I had mailed in mid-December to my aunt and uncle was returned to me. I guess it probably had to do with the fact that I failed to put their house number next to the street! Who knew??? Since they lived only a few miles away in Plainwell, Paul and I decided to hand deliver it, even though it was a few weeks late. My uncle is my dad's only living sibling out of a family of 12. Needless to say, his mind is full of stories of days gone by, and I was more than happy to listen to the tales of his childhood which included my dad-my history! Stories told of a large family, with many struggles, much love and a great faith. My uncle told of the first time he sang in church at 3 years old with my grandpa, and he has continued his love for singing for Jesus his whole life, and I remembered my dad doing the same thing. He told stories of everyone eating together. If one was late, they would all wait. Coming together as a family was of utmost importance. I soaked in the stories as I imagined my dad and his part in their family, and the importance of the thread of faith woven into their lives that has been passed down to us. As we were getting ready to leave, my uncle asked if he could pray for us, and it was so easy to grab his hands as we bowed our heads to give thanks to Jesus. I received the gift tonight of seeing the faithfulness of God in our family, through the eyes of my uncle. The blessing was mine for sure!

****

The Seal

"Sealed with a Kiss" was a popular song in the 60's. It is one that I remember singing and I still remember the chorus. It goes something like this: "So we gotta say goodbye for the summer, knowing the love we will miss, I'll send you all my love every day in a letter.... sealed with a kiss." Oh, the sadness of two young loves having to part, but writing to each other every day, kissing the envelope as they seal their undying love for each other. How romantic. I know, you are wondering why I am sharing this tidbit of nostalgia with you. Well, as I read my Bible Study this morning it spoke of the seal God has put on us as believers. He has written His love letter to us, and every day when we read it, His kisses are all over it. Why not take a moment to read His love story to us. You will no doubt enjoy the fact that unlike in the song, you will never have to part, because you are sealed with HIS LOVE.

****

The Struggle of Decisions

It is such a beautiful morning. A few years ago, Paul and I bought a small cottage on a lake about 20 minutes from our house. I guess you could say that it is our happy place. This morning I am sitting outside on the porch, drinking coffee, and looking at the lake. Water always seems to calm me. Does it have the same effect on you too? There is a quiet at the lake that is different from anywhere else. I am for a moment at peace. It's strange, though; I am still filled with the everyday cares of life. I struggle with a decision that needs to be made, wanting to make sure it is God's will and not mine, so I wrestle with the outcome. Pulling away from the noises of the world around me, I am praying that I will hear His voice more clearly. So, I will fill my mind and heart today with praise to the One who already knows my future, who knows my heart and knows my struggle. My struggle is real, but God is bigger than any struggle I face. I know in the depths of my heart that He is speaking to me in that still small voice: I have got this; you just trust Me.

****

The Disconnect

Have you ever had that feeling that you are walking around doing life as usual, but somewhere there is a disconnect? Some days I can do life and it seems that my heart is the only thing in gear, and it usually gets stomped on. Other days I go along and react with my mind, excluding anything my heart might be telling me, and that can result in hurting others. The great disconnect is in me, my mind and my heart not working in unison. I need to constantly keep my heart filled with Christ as well as my mind. When I do, He tells me I can do all things through Him, for my strength is His. Only then can I be the person He has called me to be. I guess now you all know what my struggles are today; could it be some of yours too?

****

A praying Pastor

When you attend a small church, you notice things that might be hidden to you at a bigger church. Today I was following along with the order of worship. If you have been at church recently you probably know the order: prayer, music, Scripture reading, offering and sermon. It was between the offering and sermon that I glanced over to where Pastor Mike McCrumb was sitting and I was drawn into the scene before me. All around him the service was going as expected, while he was sitting head down in communion with God. His prayer had blocked out what was going on all around him and I am sure that he was asking God to speak through him the words that we the church needed to hear. The weight of this task set before him was clearly seen in his position as he prayed. It was after church when everyone was going about saying their goodbyes when I was drawn once again to a circle of people huddled together, arms locked and heads bowed. Pastor Mike was, along with several others, again praying for a certain need of someone in his flock. I was thankful today to witness a pastor who earnestly seeks God for His wisdom, compassion and strength. Again, thanks Pastor Mike for the picture you left in my mind today.

****

So, here we are in the year 2021. Everyone seemed to look forward to leaving 2020 behind but in all reality, nothing really changed at the stroke of midnight on January 1st. It is just another day. But then again, it is another day, and I have been given this day to make a difference, I have been given this day to show love, and I have been given this day to live. 2020 was filled with change, it was filled with sorrow, it was filled with sadness and it was filled with promise. No different than any other year. Life is a mixture of joy and sorrow, laughter and loss, pain and healing, and life and death. We walk hand in hand with these everyday. If we are living, we cannot escape them. Yet, it is how we respond to them that will make the difference. I love it when my heart is filled with laughter and fun. It is easy to live life when all is good. The true test of a life lived well is when you can face those days of sickness and sorrow, pain and loss, sadness and loneliness with the knowledge that Jesus holds your everyday in His hands. What a great place to be. So 2021, I am sure you will be no different than the years before you. My hope though is that I will be able respond with patience, love and forgiveness as I come face to face with whatever the year 2021 brings. I have a feeling we will all need seat belts for the rollercoaster ride ahead of us. Hold on tight to the hands that will never let you go.

Becky's Beckonings

The Prostitute, Jesus and the religious leader, A story from Luke 7:36-50

In 16 verses today, I read a story of longing, pride, love and forgiveness, and here is what I realized. There are three main characters in this passage: Jesus, the Pharisee, (a religious man) and a prostitute.

I would say it is quite a combination of people, and yet the lesson I would learn from them needs to be studied over and over again.

Jesus was invited to a Pharisee's home for dinner. This is hospitality in action. We really don't know what his motive was when he asked Jesus to dine with him; he could have very well been trying to entrap Him. Though whatever the reason was, Jesus accepted the invitation. As Jesus was reclining at the table, the sinful woman entered.

I wonder how she knew Jesus? I doubt that she had heard Him speak in the temple; she was a prostitute. Where had she crossed paths with Him? Maybe she followed Him from afar; she probably stayed in the shadows not wanting to be noticed. At some point she must have heard Him speak. He spoke of forgiveness of sins, He spoke of peace, He spoke to her heart, and she had to follow Him. She wanted the Living Water and the Bread of Life that He spoke of. She wanted to have her thirst quenched with the Living Water and to have her hunger satisfied with the Bread of Life forever. She wanted HIM. As much as she desired Jesus, nothing could get in her way. Not religious people, not the scornful looks of others, not even a dinner party she was not invited to. She wanted Him, she wanted to be free from sin, so she invited herself in. She had to go where He was, with all she had, her perfume in a jar and herself.

I am sure as soon as she saw Him in His reclined position at the table, she knew exactly what she had to do. She knelt at His feet, and in an instant the jar of perfume she was holding began pouring out on them. Her kisses and tears combined with the perfume she poured to form an aroma pleasing to Jesus. Her hair she used to wipe His feet as her heart poured out the love she had for Him. He was the only One to bring her hope. He was what her heart and soul had been longing for.

In a group of religious people, she was the only one who understood, for with her heart and her actions rolled together in one act of love, she gave all she had.

We are called to do the same, to give our all to Him. No matter who we are or what we have done, we need to place ourselves at Jesus' feet and weep. He is the only One that can fill our souls with eternity. Let Him come in; He longs to fill your heart with Himself. He is really the only thing you will ever need. Just ask him.

The Pharisee, being a religious man, invited Jesus in for dinner. The Scripture says that Jesus was reclining at the table with them. I wonder what their conversations were about. What would mine be about if Jesus was sitting at my table? What would I do if an unwanted, uninvited and unsavory person showed up at the door carrying a jar filled with something and was headed right for the guest? I am not sure what I would do. But I do know the Bible says the Pharisee saw her. He thought to himself, "If Jesus was a prophet he would know what kind of woman this is; a sinner, a prostitute." Oh, how many times have I judged a situation incorrectly and thought to myself piously, "What are they doing?"

The Pharisee had hardly finished his thought, and Jesus answered him. Did you get that? The Pharisee thought to himself. He did not verbalize it, but Jesus knew his thoughts. WOW!! He answered him, and called him by name. "Simon." He proceeded to tell Simon a story he would understand.

Two men owed money. One owed a large amount and one owed a smaller amount. They were both forgiven of their debt. Jesus asked which one would love more. Simon responded correctly. The one who was forgiven more.

Jesus, then looking at the woman, directed Simon to look at her too. He spoke. "Do you see this woman?" I can only wonder what the Pharisee was thinking. Of course he saw this woman; he had passed judgment on her as soon as she entered his house. She was uninvited and had been a distraction ever since she entered his home.

Jesus continued to speak. He reminded Simon that when He entered his home, He was not given water to wash His feet, there were no kisses and no one poured oil on Him. Can you feel Simon sinking lower and lower with every accusation? Yet Jesus said, "This woman, since she entered has not stopped kissing my feet, pouring oil and weeping as she wiped my feet with her hair."

I wonder what was going through this woman's mind. It says in verse 44 that Jesus turned toward the woman. I don't think His eyes ever left hers. I wonder when He was speaking to Simon if that was the time her eyes might have begun to show a little sparkle. Did she at that moment know her heart was being filled with the Living Water, the Bread of Life and the Lover of her soul?

I also wonder what Simon was thinking as Jesus spoke to the woman, "Your sins are forgiven."

At this time in the story, the other guests at the party are mentioned. They whispered amongst themselves, "Who is this who forgives sins?"

The scene thankfully does not end here. Jesus has the last say as He speaks to the woman, "Your faith has saved you. Go in peace."

We are left wondering if Simon became a believer that day, or the guests. What we do know is that each one of them heard the same thing, but it was the woman that was forgiven.

The woman. She knew she was a sinner, a prostitute, and that Jesus was the only One who could save her.

The Pharisee was a religious man, upstanding in his community and church and was close enough to touch Jesus, but might not have recognized who Jesus is.

This story ends and begins with Jesus. It begins with Jesus entering a home for dinner, and ends with Jesus forgiving the intruder. The woman is not named in this story. I think it is intentional. We are all this woman. We all need to give everything we are, and everything we have to Him, because we are all sinners, in need of Jesus' saving grace. So, go ahead, be an intruder and go where you have to to find Him. Your life will never be the same.

I hope you will take time to read this story of forgiveness for yourself. It is found in Luke 7:38-50. Find out if you are the intruder, or the unbelieving invited guest.

****

A Birthday party, a dance and a head on a plate

This story in Matthew 14 was dancing in my mind on my birthday. As I reread the story I was convicted of my lack of courage.

The scene takes place at a birthday party for Herod (the man with all the power in his territory) but obviously he still wanted to have a birthday party (some things never change). I can imagine it took days to get the stage set for the birthday production. The best guests were chosen, the food cooked just right, the entertainment was ready, and I am sure the wine was ripe for drinking.

Before this scene takes place, Scripture reminds us that Herod had John the Baptist thrown in prison. Why? He spoke the truth. I guess it wasn't very popular to tell the man in charge that he should not be with his brother's wife. John had told him it was against the law. He spoke the truth and was imprisoned for it. I keep quiet about truth because I might get laughed at or mocked. I have never even been close to being imprisoned for speaking truth, but I can tell you, I have kept my mouth shut when I should have spoken out. Not John the Baptist. He pointed out sin and spoke truth in spite of what would happen to him. In verse 5, it says Herod was ready to have him killed, but he feared what the people would do because they thought him to be a prophet.

So, John is in prison as the party starts. The guests arrive, the feasting begins, and now it's time for the entertainment to capture the audience's attention. The daughter of Herodias (his brother's wife's daughter) stepped on stage. From what the Scripture says, she danced and Herod was overjoyed and grateful, so much so that he tells the young woman that she can have anything she wants. He speaks this in front of all of his guests, so he must deliver on his offer. What went through this young girl's mind? Maybe she could ask for her own palace, maybe some more jewels or a new line of fast carriages. She had just won the lottery, but her dreams of fortune were short lived when her mother tells her what to ask for.

You would think this would be a time that Herodias, being her mom, might make a wise choice for her daughter. Nope, not her! Her anger burned against John the Baptist. He was the one pointing out her sin and at that moment the only thing she wanted was his head. On a platter! I hope I never let my heart get so filled with anger for someone that I would want them dead. But isn't that what unresolved hatred and sin can do?

I have always wondered what this young daughter's response to her mom's request was. Shock? I bet that was there. Did she question her mom's choice? Did she even ask why? What we know for sure is that she went out to Herod, stood in front of him and asked for the head of John the Baptist on a platter. Herod had no choice but to grant her wish. Did he hesitate? Maybe. But earlier in the text we read that he too wanted John dead. The order was given.

We don't know if John the Baptist was told what was going to happen to him, but in the blink of an eye, or should we say the swing of an axe, he was in heaven and his head was on a platter at Herod's birthday party. Not where we would expect the forerunner of Christ to end up. We are left wondering what happens next. Was the party over when the head on a platter showed up? Whatever happened to John's head? We will never know, but this story should be our wakeup call that following Christ is not always easy. We often think if we do what Christ calls us to do, everything will be sunshine and roses. I know I do at times. But Scripture tells us a far different story. Take some time to read how most of the disciples died, or find some books on modern day martyrs. Realize we are called to follow Christ where He leads, no matter where that road might go. In John 14 Christ tells us, "In this world you will have trouble, but take heart. I have overcome the world."

****

The Birth of Christ

We all know the story surrounding the birth of Christ. I have heard it over and over as long as I can remember. The angel appears to Mary and then to Joseph, a long trip to Bethlehem, no room at the inn, a natural delivery in a stable, a host of angels, the visit from the shepherds, the visit from the wise men, and an escape to Egypt. That covers the basics.

But have you ever taken a moment to put yourself in any one of those situations, in the time period it took place? Today the news of an unwed mother wouldn't even raise an eyebrow. For Mary, it could have easily meant death. And even knowing what her fate might be, she chose life. Today, marrying someone who is pregnant with another man's baby, well, you might be considered almost honorable. For Joseph, there was ridicule and scorn, and since we know that people really haven't changed much, they were both the gossip topic of the day. But Joseph chose life too! These choices did not come without a great hardship.

What pregnant woman, ready to deliver, sets out on a hundred mile journey on a mule? Finally arriving at their destination and you feel the birth pains start. Today, no problem. You go to the hospital. For them, it was searching for a room. And none could be found. Haven't we all been a little frustrated with the innkeeper? I mean really, he turned them away. He said no room. Ummm…innkeeper…did you notice that the young woman was going to have her baby now? He still says no room. But when there are no rooms, well, there are no rooms. I have often wondered why he didn't give up his room. But would I? He must have had a bit of compassion on the couple though. He did at least offer them the stable.

I have heard this story so often that I fail to wrap my mind around the reality of delivering the baby in a dirty, smelly, unclean barn. I am pretty sure that if I was Mary, this would have been the time my doubts would kick in and I would be questioning if I had heard the angel correctly. Am I not carrying God's Son? This must have been beyond what Mary thought she could ever do. Did she feel like God had abandoned her? We get to look back at her story knowing full well that this was all part of God's plan. She didn't see that.

Funny thing is, God still does that in our lives today. We can't see why we have to go through some of the difficult times in our lives either. He has a plan for our life, and he will get us to the place He wants us so that we can bring glory to Him. We just have to keep reminding ourselves of this truth. That's what Mary did. She changed the comfort of her world to bring Jesus into the world, her Savior and ours. Maybe this year you could take time to read or reread the story of Christ's birth. Let Jesus' birth once again renew the awe and wonder of the best gift ever.

****

Ten Lessons I Learned From Philippians for a New Year

The sermon yesterday in church focused on the New Year, 2020. We were reminded to ask God to give us spiritual eyes, so that we can see clearly what His plan for our lives in 2020 will be. It made me realize how often I fail to ask God for his spiritual eyes. Then today I read Philippians. A good read as we enter into the New Year. I will be using quotes from the NIV. Paul was writing to the Philippians, but today he spoke volumes to me for the New Year.

Phil 1:6 "being confident of this, that he who began a good work in you will carry it on to completion until the day of Christ." Wow, that is encouraging. (Lesson 1) When God starts a good work in you….HE WILL FINISH IT!!!

Phil 1:9 "And this is my prayer; that your love may abound more and more in knowledge and depth of insight so that you may be able to discern what is best and may be pure and blameless until the day of Christ." (Lesson 2) God wants to fill me with his knowledge and insight. He wants me to understand HIS will.

Phil 1:21 "For to me, to live is Christ and to die is gain." (Lesson 3) I have nothing to fear in this world. I will live for Christ everyday, and when I die it is my gain. My home is not here.

Phil 2:3-4 "Do nothing out of selfish ambition or vain conceit, but in humility consider others better than yourselves. Each of you should look not only to your own interests, but to the interests of others." (Lesson 4) Get ME out of the way so I can see the needs of others. (Pretty sure I will need extra help with this one).

Phil 2:10-11 "That at the name of Jesus every knee will bow and every tongue confess that Jesus Christ is Lord, to the glory of God the Father." (Lesson 5) It doesn't matter what others say about my Jesus. All will bend a knee and verbally acknowledge that Jesus is Lord. If I am being laughed at and mocked for my faith, do not lose heart. It all works out in the end.

Phil 3:8 "What is more, I consider everything a loss compared to the surpassing greatness of knowing Christ Jesus my Lord, for whose sake I have lost all things." (Lesson 6) My focus should be knowing Christ. What else really matters?

Phil 3:13b-14 "Forgetting what is behind and straining toward what is ahead, I press on toward the goal to win the prize for which God has called me heavenward in Christ Jesus." (Lesson 7) It is time to forget my screw ups and failures and get busy doing what God has called me to.

Phil 4:4-8 "Rejoice in the Lord always, I will say it again; Rejoice! Let your gentleness be evident by all. The Lord is near. Do not be anxious about anything, but in everything by prayer and petition with thanksgiving, present your requests to God. And the peace of God that transcends all understanding will guard you hearts and minds in Christ Jesus. Finally brothers, whatever is right, whatever is pure, whatever is lovely, whatever is admirable if anything is excellent or praiseworthy--- think about such things." (Lesson 8) Learn to be thankful; God is near; quit fretting over things; pray more; praise more; focus on good!

Phil 4:12-13 "I know what it is to be in need, and I know what it is to have plenty. I have learned the secret of being content in any and every situation, whether well fed or hungry, whether living in plenty or in want. I can do everything through HIM who gives me strength." (Lesson 9) I need God's help in order to be satisfied with Him. As long as I have Him, I can do everything He calls me to do.

Phil 4:19 "And my God will meet your needs according to his glorious riches in Christ Jesus." (Lesson 10) I have nothing to worry about. Jesus will meet all my needs. I pray as I step into 2020 that I will become more of who He created me to be, that I will see with His vision, that I will be obedient to His calling as I long for the day that I will see Him face to face. 2020. Bring it on; there is nothing to fear, for God is already there.

****

Making Sense of Sanctification

I have known for a long time that I am pretty much obsessive about certain things. Books for one. I can start to read a book and nothing else gets done in my life until the last page of the book is turned. So I have learned to read when I know I have some extra time. Jigsaw puzzles bring about the same response. I can't go away and leave them until they are finished.

I was going to be at our cottage for the night, so I thought to myself, why not get out a puzzle? Little did I know that Jesus would teach me a lesson from the time I started to put the border together until the last piece was locked in place. For some reason it took me forever to get the border done. The pieces were small, and some looked like they were in the right spot, only to find out they went somewhere else. Finally, after much frustration and many sighs, I could see the border where my pieces would soon become like the picture on the box.

It was a 500-piece puzzle, it looked simple. (Don't they always when you are staring at the box?) Looking at all the pieces that went inside the frame, I realized that this might take a bit longer than I planned. Since this puzzle was purchased at a garage sale for 25 cents, I also knew there was a possibility that not all the pieces had made it back into the box, rendering an incomplete puzzle. But all the border pieces were there, so my chances were good. I set out to complete the puzzle.

As I started my puzzle adventure, there were times that I knew a piece should fit, but no matter how many times I tried to force it, it did not go where I thought it should. Then there were times that everything seemed to fit just fine and I felt pretty confident in my puzzle-working skills, until all the pieces were the same color, and I thought I would never find the perfect place for them, and so I struggled. But I was not going to quit. By then my obsession with the puzzle had kicked into high gear. You would think that the closer I came to finishing the puzzle, the easier the pieces would go in. Not the case with this one. Every time I picked up the few remaining pieces, I knew for sure I didn't have enough to finish my masterpiece. It looked like I had more empty spaces than pieces. But finally, I was looking at the complete, finished and perfect puzzle. It was at that moment, I saw before me the lesson Jesus had been teaching me. Do you see it? I am the puzzle, and so are you.

Jesus has given us a border to live within. When we live within His boundaries, (His Word) the pieces of our lives will fall into place because He is placing them in the perfect position. Oh, it won't be easy; we might think that a certain piece should be placed somewhere else, I might even wonder why one piece in my life has to be there at all. Some pieces take too long to find their rightful spot, some have to be pressed tight, and others go in easy. This does not happen overnight, it is a work that will continue until we take our last breath. But you know what, all we really need to know is that Jesus is at work creating the picture our lives will become, all the while gazing at His finished masterpiece: each one of us!

****

How Do You Measure a Life?

I am not sure why this question was floating through my mind at 2:30 a.m., because seriously at that time, I just wanted to sleep. But there it was invading my thoughts. What do I know about the measure of life? Absolutely nothing! Or so I thought. Do we measure life only in the length of days we live on this earth? The longer we live does give us an advantage just from the sheer length of days we live. We can use those days to help others, or we can waste them. In my 65 years on this earth, I have managed to do both. So can we measure life by the number of days lived?

A child that is born alive but dies soon after their birth, is their life measured in the amount of breaths taken? Or do they matter at all?

Or what about the person who suffers from mental disease and is institutionalized most of their lives and can contribute nothing to society. How do we measure their life?

And that is what I struggled with at 2:30 in the morning…and this is where my question was answered.

I have come to realize that God is the One that gives us value. We are created in His image, and we are all His image bearers. That's it. Not how long we live on this earth, not how many breaths we take, not whether we function well in society. It is because He creates life, that is why my life has value and so does yours. He created me for a purpose. He tells me in His Word that when I seek Him with my whole heart, I will be found by Him. When I find Him and see my value because of what He did for me, therein is where we find how life should be measured. There is absolutely nothing I can do to earn this; it has all been done for me. Every one of us has value and every life has been created for a purpose. I hope each of you can see how your life has value. Not for what you can or cannot do, but for what He has already done! FYI...tonight, I just want to sleep!

****

Sins Forgiven

Today while I was in the middle of my Bible Study lesson and knowing I am one day behind, and doing things in a hurry as usual, I was stopped in my tracks as I could see in my mind a list of my sins, staring at me. This list was on a piece of paper with each sin lined up on the left side of the paper, and they went all the way down.

I knew what it was...and I shuddered. I began to wonder why God would even take a second to look at me, let alone love me. As I looked down the page at my sins, I noticed on the right side of the page was one name. It was the only thing on that side of the page. It was Jesus! The picture is so clear in my mind...Jesus. My list of sins on one side; His name on the other.

Then I looked at my Bible already open to 1 John 3:1 and I read: "How great is the love the Father has lavished on us, that we should be called children of God, and that is what we are." Wow, He knows me! He sees all of my sins, and still lavishes His love on me, and calls me HIS child. The side of the page showing my sins is folded under and covering them is Jesus! It was a good Bible study morning.

****

John 8:1-11 The Woman Caught...and Released!! Hope you enjoy the read.

I knew it was wrong. I knew I could be killed for what I was about to do. No one will find out. It's night and everyone else is sleeping, and I am lonely. I let my mind over ride what I knew I shouldn't do. I gave in to my fleshly desire and sought the companionship of someone I was not married to. I kept telling myself that no one will ever find out, but I still knew it was wrong.

In an instant my home was being invaded. I was being dragged out of the very place I thought I could be safe. I barely had any time to grab my clothes, let alone a covering for my bare body. I was grabbed and dragged, but only me. Where is the man I was with?

142

Why am I the only one standing before this crowd of men? I realized then, as I searched the eyes of my accusers that I would die very soon. The men stood there looking at me with disgust and arrogance, just waiting for the right moment to throw the stones they were aching to release from their hands.

I heard them tell the one they call Teacher, "This woman was caught in the act of adultery". They were right; I could not even begin to deny what was so obvious to all of them. They continued on, "In the Law, Moses commanded us to stone such a woman. Now what do you say?" I am trying to look at this man they call Teacher, but my shame is so great I can only look to the ground. I knew this would be the last thing I would see before I exited this world, for what the Pharisees and teachers of the law said was   true. Stoning is what I deserved. But this man, the one they called teacher, started to write on the ground with his finger. I don't know what he was writing. What I do know is He stood up and said to them, "If any one of you is without sin, let him be the first one to throw the stone at her."

He then stooped over again, continuing his writing. I knew what was coming. I waited to feel the stones hit my body. I crouched to protect myself from what I knew would be a painful death. But there was nothing. My tears were falling from the realization there were no rocks being thrown. It became very quiet, when moments before the men were in a fury of making sure the law was kept. I noticed the "Teacher" stoop to write again on the ground. As he was writing, I heard the first of many stones being dropped to the ground. Not all at once, but a few at a time. The crowd of men were no longer surrounding me.

I had no idea what was going on. I was looking at a circle of rocks that a few moments before would have caused my death but are now just a reminder of my sin and something I would soon learn called "Grace". I heard the one they called Teacher say to me, "Woman, where are they? Has no one condemned you?" I replied in the only words that would escape from my lips, "No one, sir". The teacher's response, "Then neither do I condemn you". Wait, I deserve to be stoned, my life is filled with sin. Who is this man who has told me He didn't condemn me? Then, He spoke once more, words that I will hear forever in my mind. "Go now and leave your life of sin." I had just been handed my life back. I should be dead. Who is this Teacher? I don't know who He is, but I want to spend the rest of my life pleasing Him. I hope you will too.

****

The Healing at the Pool...

I am there right in the Bible, but you don't know my name. My name really isn't that important, but what Jesus did for me, now THAT is what is important. My whole life was spent laying by the pool near the Sheep Gate. That is where you go when you have something wrong with you. Trust me, I was never alone there. I had the company of the blind, the lame and the paralyzed. I have seen it all. I know that sometimes when the water is stirred, people get healed. But not me, I can't move by myself. And so far, no one has come to help me.

Thirty-eight years of despair. You get used to people going by and not even looking at you. Of course, I don't really blame them. Who wants to look at us? A group of people that are useless. That was before I met Jesus. Of course, at that time I didn't know who He was.   He was just another face that glanced our way. But today, this man came right up to where I was laying and he asked me "Do you want to get well?" Someone was speaking to me! I said, "Sir, I have no one to help me into the pool when the water is stirred. While I am trying to get in, someone else goes down ahead of me." Oh, why did I respond with that? Why didn't I just say YES!!

He could have left me after my ridiculous response, but this man said something that will echo in my mind for eternity. This time I sensed a power behind His words when He spoke that demanded a response. I had never heard a command so direct before. "Get up! Pick up your mat and walk." There was no time to think about it, there was no time to practice getting up, there was only a command I knew I had to follow. And I got up! I bent over and picked up my mat and WALKED! My legs were not weak, they were not sore from thirty-eight years of no movement, they were strong, I was healed. Not over a period of time, but in an instant as soon as the words were out of his mouth. I did what He said. I was changed on the outside and now I am walking!

Of all days to be healed…it was a Sabbath day. The Jews that were in the area saw me carrying my mat and told me it was against the law for me to carry my mat. I was quick to respond to them, "The man who made me well told me to pick up my mat and walk."

(I think the Jews were way more interested in following the law than in rejoicing in a man's healing.)

They also wanted to know who told me to pick up my mat and walk. I told them the truth. I had no clue who He was, for once He commanded me to walk, He just slipped into the crowd and was gone.

It was later that day when the same man found me at the temple, and He said, "See, you are well again, now stop sinning or something worse may happen to you." It was then that I realized my body had been healed earlier in the day by this man, but in the temple later that day, my eyes saw Who healed my broken soul. Of course, then I knew Who the man was and I went away quickly and told the Jews. "It was Jesus Who made me well."

Why not read the story for yourself today? John 5:1-15

Things to ponder:

Why would Jesus command this man to pick up his mat, knowing it was against the law?

Why did Jesus go out of His way to find this man when He had already healed his body?

Why didn't the man who was healed go in search of the One who healed him?

The spoken Word brought healing to his body for a time, and the spoken Word healed his soul for eternity.

Physical healing of the body is not enough.

Jesus never gives up searching for us.

Life on the Gray Side

Public restrooms

In my 64 years on this earth I can say I have seen and used many. I'm sure you can say the same thing. It should be a simple process. In my home, I have to pump the soap dispenser to get soap, my hand towel is ready at a moment's notice to be grabbed off the holder, and my toilet has a handle for me to flush. I know how to do it. Upon entering any public restroom today, you never know what to expect. Do your business, get up from the toilet, and look around to flush. No handle, but no flushing going on either. What do you do? Take two steps to the door and it flushes. Is there an electronic eye that waits until it sees the total frustration in your eyes, and then flushes? But of course now we are only getting started on the fun in the next quest as we go to wash our hands. Hmmm. No handles on the faucet. OK, here comes the magic water; but wait, it is not coming out. Wave your hands back and forth under the faucet. Nothing. I think it must be that same electronic eye that captured my moment of frustration in the stall that is waiting until I reach that same crazed look, and then releases the water. By this time, a process that should take only a few minutes is taking more time than you could have thought possible, and you still have to get the soap out of the dispenser. So, you hold your hand under the soap unit, and wait, and wait and wait. So far, everything else in here is an "I'll do it for you kind of place "so I wait. No soap! Oh, there it is. A button. I am supposed to press this button to get my soap. Wow, it works. Now I have soap, water and clean wet hands. There they are. Towel holders on the wall. Again, I try to decide if this is the do it yourself one, or one that I must wave my hands frantically underneath to get a towel? There seems to be a large dial on the side of the dispenser. So I quit waving my wet hands under the unit and reach up and turn it, and like magic, my towel appears. I breathe a sigh of relief knowing I have finally mastered another public restroom. And I also realize that since this process has taken longer than I ever thought, yes, you guessed it. I have to start all over again!!!

****

Getting Older

Yes, it happened, in a way that everything seems to be happening these days, fast and furious. Today I got another year older. Now, there are some perks to being 63. You don't get carded for Senior Discounts; for that matter, you don't even have to ask for the discount. One look by the twenty-something server is enough to get it deducted from your bill immediately. You get pretty excited by the smaller things in life, like still being able to balance yourself on one leg while you try to get your jeans on, or when you stop and talk to someone and you really do remember their name, or how about refraining from telling a story everyone has heard from you a million times; now that is control! Yes, that is the life of being 63. But the joy of my life is not in the things I can or can't do anymore. Rather it's in the people that surround me with love, those that will be standing alongside of me when I walk through rough waters, those that make me laugh till I cry, and when I'm crying, they can somehow make me laugh. I can say without hesitation that I have been blessed for 63 years with many of these people. They are you, my family and friends. I can't wait to see what God has planned for me this year. I know it will be an adventure. Let the fun begin. Life on the Gray Side...here I come.

****

Nail Polish and the car

How many of you have heard the old wives tale that people you know die in groups of three? I have no idea where it came from or the validity of it, it's just a phrase I have heard many times. Today, my new phrase is going to be "Life on the Gray Side" comes in droves! Oh, do I wish it would stop at three; but it is a never ending story. My first entry into the Gray Side this week came on Sunday morning. We left the house earlier for church than usual, and I still needed to touch up the nail polish on my toes. In my early morning mind I thought I would do it in the car at church. Problem solved! When you're in the car doing your toe nails, bending is a requirement and yes I can still do it. What I didn't expect was the nail polish brush dropping a big glob of polish right below my nail. I was looking at a glob of bright red polish as it was quickly drying on my skin. Grabbing a napkin from the glove box, I started to blot the polish. It came off, but left a bright red round circle below the nail. Remember I said a glob of polish, most of which was now on the napkin...or so I thought. No, it had managed to seep through the napkin and made a home on the inside of my hand, along with a bright red coating on the back of my ring! So now my toe has a bright red blob, my hands are red, and at that moment the Pastor taps on my window to say good morning! I respond with a good morning too and I share with him that I am in the middle of writing another story for the Gray Side! He doesn't have any idea what I am in the middle of. My mind at this point is trying to figure out just how I am going to get the red polish off my toe and hand. I didn't think to bring polish remover. But there in the church kitchen, on the counter, I spot a bottle of Fantastic! Why not? It is worth a try so I squirted my toe and hand with a household cleanser and scrubbed...and it worked!!! My hand and toe have never been as sanitized. I am sure they will never be quite the same again, and I am also sure I will never try to put nail polish on in the car again. I am sure my life on the Gray Side is just getting warmed up this week-episode 2 to follow!

****

Bees and The Gray Side

When "Life on the Gray Side" comes face to face with a lesson in life, I can do nothing more than sit back, laugh and learn. My story starts last week, when a mentor at the Center tried to open the door with a bee on the knob. She yelled, the bee fell, and I watched. She had been stung by that pesky bee, and her hand of course started to swell. The bee was vicious. Fast forward a week. I am getting ready to enter the Center, knowing full well there is a swarm of bees that love trying to get in the door with me. I made sure I kept my eye on them, as I shooed them away. Oh, but guess where I failed to look? You are right, the door knob. My hand grabbed that knob just about the same time a bee was landing there (or maybe it was waiting for me). Either way, I yelled, the bee fell and my thumb started to look like it belonged on the hand of a giant. I got in the door and noticed the bee trying to crawl away. Nothing doing. I stepped on him, gently though. NOT! I had killed the bee that had caused my pain. I kept thinking there is a hidden lesson here, and then it dawned on me. All the while I had my mind focused on the obvious problem, the swarming bees on the door, but I had failed to see or even look at the hidden problem, the one that got me. Isn't it like that in life? We spend all our time fighting and focusing on the obvious problems, when in reality it is the ones in hiding that will cause us the most harm. So today, keep your eyes open to the real dangers. They will come from the least place you expect. Living life on "The Gray Side" doesn't mean you stop learning, but it does mean you have to make room for lots of laughter. Enjoy your day!

****

My House: the new "Mystery Spot"

How many of you have taken a walk through the "Mystery Spot" in the U.P.? I remember enjoying my first trip there as a kid. I couldn't figure out the crazy stuff happening right before my eyes. Fast forward to today. I seriously think I am living in my own "Mystery Spot." Yes, soon and very soon, this house will be open for business. Heck- it won't even cost you much to enter, and you might even be involved in solving the many mysteries this house holds. Your detective skills will be used as you search for lost items. Some will reappear without notice in places where you would not think to look. Yes, there is that check that was on the table last night, and this morning was gone. Even though I searched in everything and everywhere, it was nowhere to be found. (Except later I found out that Paul had put it in the desk, the only place I did not look). The case of the missing banana is still on the books but is now listed as a cold case. Clothes that have vanished, tools that have been put away, never to be found again will be on the list for searchers to find. Oh, and I must not forget those things that I meant to hide, and have totally forgotten where I hid them. I did learn my lesson on that one. After the age of 50, .do not,

I repeat, do not hide anything; it will never be found again. It seems like only yesterday that the "Mystery Spot" of my youth brought so much joy, and yet the "Mystery Spot" on the "Gray Side" is something that must be reckoned with. I find it frustrating and also a bit funny at the same time, but it is what it is. Watch for the "Open" sign on the front door. It will be there soon. Well, as soon as I can find it.

****

The mind is an interesting thing.

Today I challenged mine, and it lost! It was lost the moment it said, "You can do it." Famous last words. Today I arrived early for my morning walk, and as I approached the parking lot of the church, I realized it had not been plowed. Hmmm...a truck track appeared to have gone around the lot and circled up to the door. In that split second my mind tricked me, knowing full well that I have a little car, but I could surely follow those big tracks and arrive at a spot in front of the door. (Lie of the mind#1) As I started to follow the tracks, I was pretty confident, until they disappeared under piles of blown snow! Well, there is only one thing to do now, back up and follow the same tracks that led me to this dilemma. Okay, you can do this. (Lie of the mind #2) Backing up has never been my strong suit, and today I learned that truth again. As I started backing up, you all know what I did, don't you? Yup, I got off those tracks quickly, and was stuck! Of course, in that situation I did what any wife would do. I called my husband. Paul is always patient with me, but today I could tell by the look he gave me that I was pushing the edge of it. And when he spoke those wise words to me, "You did notice it wasn't plowed, right?" it was then that I knew: A mind is a terrible thing to waste. I will try not to let mine lie to me again. (Lie of the mind #3) Enjoy your day, and stay out of unplowed parking lots.

****

Just another typical day in the life of a 63-year-old living "Life on The Gray Side."

I had some coffee creamer in my car to bring to the Women's Center today. Of course, I put it on the floor, just in case there was some leakage. And sure enough, as I went to retrieve it, there it was, a small drip of creamer on my car mat. Well, not wanting to have my car smell like coffee creamer, I reached into the glove box to get a napkin to clean it up. Simple, right? Not really.

Now if you can, imagine me sitting in the driver's seat, squirming under the steering wheel, trying to reach this little spot on my car mat that I just couldn't get. Most people, when they couldn't reach it this way, would have the common sense to get out of the car, walk around to the passenger side, open the door and reach in and clean it. But as you all know I am not most people. So I stretched and crunched and reached trying to get that darn spill off my car mat. Then I heard it, a glub, glub, glub sound. Yes, all the while I was trying to get that speck off the floor mat, I was leaning on the very container of creamer that caused this problem in the first place. And now I am seeing that my whole passenger seat, all the bags that were on the seat, and some of me, were loaded with coffee creamer. The bottle was empty. I'm sure there is a moral to this story, you know, trying to fix something small while you are creating a bigger mess. But you know for me, it will just get put into one of the many files that I am keeping. This one is labeled "Life on The Gray Side," the never-ending story.

****

The Yearly Birthday

I am not sure why at the age of 65 I am reflecting on life so much more. I guess I am at that age that you

start to see yourself as you are. There is no hiding those extra pounds that have somehow managed to show up on a body that is already trying to hide the weight that never quite came off after the birth of children. And that railing on the steps that you hardly ever held on to is now your best friend as you go up and down the stairs. You grasp it tight and hope it will hold you as you pull yourself up that long stairway, and you are equally happy that it is there to guide you safely down. There was a time that I could slip into a pair of jeans without a thought of having something to grab onto. Yes, I was able to lift one leg up and slip it into the leg of my jeans, as I so gracefully balanced on the other leg. What the heck happened to my balance? Oh, and the mirrors in my house also play tricks on me. I walk past one and take a look and wonder why my mom is staring back at me. Just when did that switch take place? I once spouted a head full of long brown hair and for the life of me, I am unable to find even one brown hair on my head. I used to laugh at those single gray hairs that would lie under all that brown hair; guess who's laughing now? Tell me, how does a face that once was smooth and clear become lined with wrinkles and spots? My mind remembers things from years ago, but I can't tell you what I did last weekend without deep thought, and then sometimes I still can't remember. This aging process is not for the faint of heart, and it is not for the casual on-looker. It is where I am now. There is not an option for a do over, only a path that leads to more aging. Funny thing is, with all that is changing around me and in me I am blessed to walk this path set before me. In all its uncertainty, in all its frustrations, in all its joys I know that God has laid the path I walk, and I know He walks it with me. So, I will continue to laugh at myself in this aging process. I have to because we all know laughter is good medicine.

****

My own Comedy Routine

In the past I have made comments that a nursing home would be a great place to get material for a comedy routine. I am not making fun of those in nursing homes, but I have run across some pretty funny happenings as I have visited friends and family that were living there. Today, that has all gone out the window when I realized I am my own best comedy material. Case in point: Friday mornings at 8:00, you will find me having breakfast with friends. We have done this for several years now. It has become routine. As usual, this morning I was not running late, but I was pushing it, as I ran around getting ready to go out the door. I do a mental check to make sure I don't forget anything. Shoes? Check. Coat? Check. Glasses? I am sure I left them upstairs the night before along with my watch. I run (well, not really run) up the stairs to check the kitchen table where I am sure I left them. Not there. Oh, yeah, I must have taken them off and laid them on the counter in the bathroom the night before. Gee, not there either. Okay, they must be downstairs. I just didn't see them. I am sure by now you have already guessed it. As I was heading down the stairs, I realized that they were on my face. And my watch was already on my wrist. So, where were those pesky glasses this morning? Who knows? I only know that at some point, I placed them on my head and put my watch on, and have absolutely no recollection of doing it. I did make it to breakfast on time, and I also have another story to add to my "Life on The Gray Side" file. This is also giving my kids and Paul the evidence they need to have me placed in one of the nursing homes when I am not looking! If I come up missing, look for me. I am sure I will be in the home that has the upstairs light on, but no one is there.

****

Well, it seems that this morning I had to admit to myself that I am really heading into "Life on the Gray Side."

I have been dodging the fact for some time now. Experiencing small aches and twinges on my body where none used to be, quite often finding myself saying, "What did you say?" and today, there it was- the drool. For a while now there has been the dropping of food on the clothing I am wearing while I am eating. I

154

haven't figured out why this is happening to me on a regular basis. My mouth is still in the same place on my face, my arms haven't grown in length, and the utensils I am using are the same size. So, why is this becoming a new obstacle that I must deal with? It's the curse of Life on the Gray Side, and this morning I knew I reached it. As I got ready for church, dressed in a sweater with a large collar, I brushed my teeth. Most of you are thinking no big deal!!! But that's when I noticed it. Yup, right in the center of the large collar was the toothpaste drool! I swear, I have brushed my teeth the same way for years, never had a problem before, but today that all changed. A blob of white on a blue sweater. It was like that big drool of toothpaste was laughing at me. So I laughed too, knowing this is just a glimpse of the fun that is to come, as I have safely arrived in "Life on the Gray Side."

****

It happened again! (Any time you see me start with those words you should know that my Life on The Gray Side escapades are on a roll again).

A few weeks ago, I was looking forward to seeing some people that I hadn't seen in a long time. Arriving for dinner we signed in, and the person signing us in immediately knew me! "Don't you remember me?" "Oh yes, for sure!" was my response. (I didn't have a clue). We talked a bit and then I noticed a person I recognized. Being me, I went up to her with a hug, and asked the usual questions you say to someone who you haven't seen in a long time. It was so good to see her again. We parted and I went to order our food. And there she was! The person who I thought I knew when I walked in! You guessed it. I had hugged and chatted with someone I had no idea who it was. I felt like a complete goof! Thankfully, I never ran into her again that evening, probably because I stayed at the table after that. But one thing I am sure of. I bet there is one lady telling all her friends tonight about the gray haired lady that has dementia and likes to hug. And I know she must be laughing. The same as me now! Although it did take a couple of weeks for me to get to laughter.

****

Writer's Block? No Way.

I have heard about writer's block and I am now sure that the people who suffer from it are under the age of 40. Because anyone over 40 knows that everyday life is filled with enough material to write chapter after chapter of a bestselling book. These stories are just screaming to be put down in print. Most, though, don't like to admit they are living a bestselling comedy in their daily lives. I have decided to put mine down for the whole world (at least my Facebook friends and you) to see. It was time to get my car washed. I always get a little nervous about approaching the entry of the wash. Attempting to get my tires lined up with that narrow little metal piece on the floor so I can be taken into the fun of the car wash, I always wonder if my tire is going to go in the center or off to either side. The attendant stands there with this impatient blank look on his face, with his hand motioning me forward, which tells me nothing about my tires. What I want to know is if I go forward, am I going to hit the metal track or not. His face beckons me forward. I move ahead, and thankfully I am in the exact spot I am supposed to be. I have been successful so far. I roll down my window, tell the attendant what kind of wash I want, money is exchanged, I am almost set. He then tells me to put my car in neutral. No problem. Have you ever been somewhere when you are parked and the car beside you backs up, and you get the feeling that you are the one backing up? Your stomach jumps, you grab the wheel and start to put on the brakes and then you realize you are not moving. Well, that was what happened as I started the car wash. I thought I had put it in neutral, and I had that interesting feeling about moving backward. Except you guessed it, I really was moving back. In my best car wash manners, I must have skipped right over neutral and yes, landed in reverse. In an instant, the man who had almost no expression on his face when motioning me into the car wash became very animated with his face close to my window saying, "I said neutral!" I got it. I quickly put the car in neutral, and proceeded to finish the wash. I have to say I smiled a bit to myself as I was in the car wash tunnel. I certainly gave the attendant a chance to get his blood pressure up, and I am sure the person in the car behind me was glad when I finally exited the wash. It's just another file in my "Life on the Gray Side." Heck, soon I will have enough chapters for a best seller. Who am I kidding? I already do! All in all, it was a good day.

****

We All Need to Laugh

One thing I have discovered in the past few months is that this world needs more laughter. We live in a time where our focus is always on what is going wrong in the world. I get it. There is a lot going on. But just so you know this is where I come in. Yes, even in the craziness of this world, my "Life on the Gray Side" is giving me one reminder after another that laughter is the only way I can make it through. It started this morning as I was trying to get a necklace on. Men, this one will most likely not apply to you, but seriously, just how in the heck are we supposed to get a necklace on? They have on one end a tiny little circle on the chain, and you have to hold back the clasp on the other end as you insert the tiny circle into the clasp. All this is being done behind your neck, unseen by your eyes, and held by hands that have long lost that steadiness of years gone by. I kid you not, I worked at that necklace for a few minutes and it finally made the connection so it was not going to fall off. Yes, I had accomplished what I set out to do. It took one look in the mirror to discover I had it on backwards and I had to start the process all over again. I now realize the reason older women wear longer necklaces is because they can just slip them over their heads, and forego the fight of the tiny chain versus the fat fingers and unsteady hands. Then it was on to voting. As I pulled up in the parking lot, I noticed a friend whom I had not seen in a long time, so I rolled down the passenger window to talk with her. We talked a bit, catching up on each other's lives. She then went to her car, and I went in to vote. I decided to leave my purse in the car and just take my key fob with me along with my ID, so I locked the car door and went in and voted. Returning to my car, I couldn't believe what I had done. Yes, there was my purse on the passenger side seat, and my car securely locked, with my passenger side window all the way down. Seems when I was talking to my friend, I never put the window back up. Thankfully, my purse was still there, my necklace was on the right way, and I had a couple of laughs today. "Life on the Gray Side" is showing itself just a bit more often than I'd like to admit, but I hope I helped one of you smile a bit.

****

The New Gadget

A while ago, (in my world that could be several years ago, or it could be last week), I saw a commercial about this curved piece of hard plastic that when you stepped on it, you could twist your life into slender living. I thought at the time it just looked fun. Well, on Friday while I was checking out the sales I found one! And for just $3 that piece of plastic could be mine, and I could envision myself in the Senior Olympics of twisting! I of course bought it! Fast forward to Friday evening. My piece of plastic in hand, I set out to see how this would work.

Hmm. Placing each foot at the ends of the board, all the while you are supposed to BALANCE and twist at the same time. Well, let me tell you, balance is one of those things that when you reach "Life on the Gray Side", it is not as fine tuned as it used to be, but I did it! One twist and I was grabbing for the chair to block my fall, but I am not a quitter. I tried it again, and my dreams of an Olympic medal fell to the floor, right along with me! I happened to glance on the board and see its name. Seriously, its name is Fit board! I figured out right then that you must be fit before taking on this easy, twisty, fit board. I have found a good use for it though. The curve in the board fits nicely on my head and it has two slots on each end to hold securely over my head in case of falling rocks. Always be prepared!

****

Vacations and Photos

Today I realized that I have been doing Life on the Gray Side before I was gray. I hate to admit it, but it is true. Summer is the time for vacations, right? Well a few years ago, okay more than 10, Paul and I decided to go to Boston. He had family living there and we were going to visit. I have always thought getting ready for a vacation is almost as fun as the vacation itself, so for a week or so, I was getting excited to visit a city I had never been to before. The day we left, I was ready and a bit silly. I was taking pictures at almost every road stop. I had to document every step of our trip. I had this bright idea as we stopped for a bathroom break that I would capture Paul on camera as he exited the porta john. Yes, I know you are thinking that is a bit strange, but if you know me well, it shouldn't surprise you that much. Anyway, I waited, camera in focus, pointed straight at the door. The door opens, my camera and I are ready and I shoot the best picture of a man that I have never seen before as he exits the bathroom. There I was, caught red handed, photographing a stranger, at a bathroom no less. As soon as I snapped the picture, Paul steps out of the porta john right next to the one I thought he was in. I was embarrassed to say the least, and I am sure that guy is wondering to this day why a strange woman was taking his picture as he left the bathroom. I probably should have explained myself, but I didn't. I probably should have apologized, but I didn't; what I did do was laugh during that trip every time I saw a porta john. And you know, it still made me laugh today. Oh for the fun of the pre gray days. Lesson learned: If you're going to document a vacation with photos, make sure you know it is family in the family album!

✳✳✳✳✳✳✳✳✳✳✳

The yearly Birthday...again

When you have traveled around the sun 66 times, it is definitely a time for reflection, and a bit of reminiscing. I have been doing a bit of both lately. Just when and how did I get from birth to 66 in a blink? Seriously, yesterday it seems like I was dressing up for Halloween with my siblings, and today my grand kids think they are too old to trick or treat. Yesterday, I was a teenager laying out in the sun with baby oil lathered all over, and today I ain't laying out in a bathing suit in any kind of weather. Yesterday, my biggest worry was forgetting my locker combination; today I frequently forget my keys to our house. Yesterday, hanging out with my friends was the best; today thankfully some things never change. Yesterday, I worried about being a good parent; today I get to encourage others on this same journey. Yesterday, I worried about what others thought; today I am okay with who I am. Yesterday, life was hard at times; today it still can be. Life isn't for sissies. Yesterday, I was young; today in my mind I can visit the days of my youth and smile. Yesterday, I wanted to be grown-up; today I hope I have achieved a semblance of that status. Yesterday, I thought this thing called life was a lonely highway; today I know that God has walked with me every step of the way. I was never alone. He is the same yesterday, today and forever and He keeps His promises. Can you believe it has only taken me 66 years to learn that? I hope I have a few more years to live what I have finally learned, but I know without a doubt that whatever my future holds, it is secure in Jesus. Looking back always makes me appreciate just how far I have come and a realization of how far I have yet to go. One thing is for sure. My "Life on the Gray Side" will continue to thrive and probably grow right along with me. Here's to an exciting year!

****

When the Gray Side and Communion Clash

Who said learning to laugh at one's self is healthy? I'll call this Communion Sunday or my most embarrassing moment #365. It all started out as a normal communion time: Standing in line, waiting for my turn to pull a piece of bread from the loaf held by the server of the day. It was soon my turn to dip the bread into the glass of grape juice held by the other server. I have done this on a regular basis since I was twelve, I know how it works. But this time was different. I dipped my bread, and accidently dropped it back in the glass. Now, I have to say, this is the exact moment where all reasoning and rational thinking left my mind. And I thought instantly of the five second rule. You drop it, you get it out. My bread was floating in a sea of grape juice waiting to be rescued, and yes, I did it. Without thought of those waiting in line to dip their bread, without thought of anything except getting my bread, I reached my fingers into the glass and retrieved the bread. It was a soggy mess by this time, but I got it, and finished my communion. Kneeling at the altar in prayer is when my mind kicked into a replay of what had just happened. I can tell you I lingered a little longer there, thinking to myself oh no, how could you do that, what were you thinking. Some of you are probably saying the same thing. Some of you are finding it amusing; I even think God may have smiled a little too. For me, I'm just going to catalog it in my "Living Live on the Gray Side" file. To be honest with you, the older I get, it is filling up faster than I could have even imagined.

****

Sunday proved to be a "Gray Side Day" for sure, but how was I to know that Monday would top the nail polish incident ten times over. Monday! Need I say more? It started out good. I walked with a friend, had breakfast with family and did a few chores around the house. After dinner I decided to keep up the pace and I went out to clean up around our pool area. Toys and goggles put away for another season. It was then I realized I had not checked the mail. I had this bright idea of doing a pep step to the mailbox. (How many of you remember the pep step craze?) Now mind you, I have been doing this walking thing for 65 years, and I know how it is done. One foot in front of the other, going forward to get me to my destination. Our driveway is straight, nothing to cause a problem, or so I thought. I am half way down the drive, (nothing there to cause any problems) so why did my ankle make a sharp move to the side, making me lose the balance that is already off center anyway? I have no idea. What I do know is that in a blink of an eye, I was on the ground with a pain in my ankle that warned me I might need some help getting up from this interesting situation. So, I called for Paul, who was thankfully outside working on a car. Okay, maybe it was a loud call for him, as he heard it above the running vehicle and came to my aid. By this time, I am trying to figure out just what happened. There was absolutely nothing to make me trip. Did the ground open for a second and make me tumble? Did the ankle just decide to take a break without telling me? These things I will continue to ponder, as my leg is elevated as my ankle can't bear much weight. "Life on the Gray Side" keeps me humble, but always laughing. What else can ya do?

****

Life on "The Gray Side" has struck again.

I have been doing pretty good staying under the radar when it comes to those glaring, blatant and down right ridiculous stunts that usually fill my life. But today, it caught up with me again. After a day filled with shopping, I had a car loaded with gifts, groceries, and goodies. I had been a successful shopper. Knowing I needed to stop at the bank and make a deposit, I pulled into the bank line, and thankfully got right in. I filled out my deposit slip. All is well so far. I rolled down my window and reached for the little tube to shoot my deposit over to the teller. Again, this is routine, I got this. And, I wait. There was time to balance my checkbook, listen to a song, watch the next car leave and another one arrive. I have patience but I was wondering what was going on. It seemed to be taking longer than usual. So I looked over to the bank window to see if the teller was working on my deposit, and she wasn't. But I did notice a look in her eye that told me something wasn't quite right. I glanced over to the tube that I had so carefully put in five minutes earlier and there it was. Still waiting to be sent over. I quickly pushed the send button, and the nice teller appeared on the screen saying she would take care of it right away. And she did. I wonder though, if her conversation tonight is going to be about a gray haired lady that sat forever in the bank line doing everything but sending her deposit over. What would have made the situation even more fun: I should have had some silver tinsel hanging from my gray hair.

That would have been the teller's cue, that I truly am living life on "The Gray Side."

****

So here we are the first week of 2021 and my "Life on the Gray Side" is in full swing. I try as hard as I can to keep this part of my life from showing up, but when I least expect it, it appears in full force and gets my attention once again. I always order a calendar each year for my wall in the kitchen. Each year I pick a different kind. This year I picked out one with Folk Art. It arrived in November, and I tucked it away till I needed it. I really never gave it another thought and it was proudly put in the holder on New Year's Day. While sitting at the table having lunch today, I happened to look up at my new calendar. The picture was really cute, but I noticed it said that New Year's Day was on a Wednesday. Now how can that be? I am pretty sure it was just this past Friday. Then my eyes gazed at the year on top of the calendar, and guess what? It said 2020!!!! Did I love the year 2020 so much that I bought a calendar so I could go over each date again? I think not. So why in the world did I order a calendar for last year, when I needed one for this year? That is the question I will be pondering as I place my order for a new 2021 calendar. Anyone out there want a new calendar for 2020? I have the perfect one for you. It is slightly used, but almost like new. Life on the Gray Side...you're killing me!

****

Living life on "The Gray Side" is mostly fun, but often ends up in the realm of should I say "challenging" at times. I realized that there are things I don't do anymore. How many of you women can maneuver a leg razor while standing in the shower? Well, I can't. The balance is gone. Bending over to shave to get that clean look on the leg, all the while the water showering down on you just doesn't happen in my house anymore. So, the bathtub is my main mode of cleaning and shaving. I am living this life on the "Gray Side" because it seems like all of the hair on my body has turned that color except for the legs and under arms. They are still as dark as ever and scream to be shaved on a regular basis. So, I shave them. And I thought I was doing a pretty good job, until I was sitting in the doctor's office. I had my legs crossed so the back of my leg was visible to me in a brightly lit room. To my horror, I noticed that there was a perfect strip of dark hair going down the back of my leg that somehow had missed the razor. Now by the looks of the hair on my leg, the razor has missed this area quite often. It wasn't long enough to put a hair tie in it, but I bet a bobby pin (if you live on the gray side you know what those are) would have done the job. So, again I sigh and laugh at myself, because I know this "Life on the Gray Side" is staying with me for a while so I guess I will just continue to smile.

****

It just doesn't stop. Yes, my life on The Gray Side has been showing its ugly roots again.

It wasn't enough last week that my sprayer in my kitchen sink got stuck in the on position, and I not only once but twice turned the faucet on and sprayed myself in the face both times. It wasn't enough to find myself driving past the exact place I was supposed to be, after explicitly reminding myself over and over in my mind to stop there, and doing the same thing at the next place I was going. My mind reminds me, and the gray side ignores it. But I have to tell you early this morning The Gray Side of life really took the cake. There are certain times when I have trouble sleeping, and last night I was awake most of the night. Frustrated that I couldn't sleep, along with staring at mindless TV, watching as the minutes turned to hours, finally, sleep arrived. But then as soon as it arrived, so did the nightly bathroom urge. So, dragging myself to the bathroom in a dream-like state I managed to get my business done. I just wanted SLEEP! Well, somehow in my desire to get back to my awaiting bed, I turned too soon while exiting the bathroom, and my toes caught between the bottom of the door and the floor, and the side of the door came back to hit me. I let out a cry (well, maybe it was more like a wild coyote scream) and hobbled back to bed. And I went to sleep, with a throbbing in my toes and a sore chest. Fast forward to morning. As my foot hit the floor my mind remembered my dangerous dance with the door a few hours before, and again I let out that coyote yell, as I felt a streak of pain from my toes. Hobbling to get to my closet and with each pained step I took, I decided I better laugh at this because I think that there is probably going to be a life filled with "Life on The Gray Side" moments. Hopefully, these moments, as frustrating, painful and downright humiliating as they are, will be met with a smile and a hope of knowing the best is yet to come! It is the first bone I have broken.

Enjoy your day.

****

Life sure has been different for the last few months, but just so you all know "My Life on the Gray Side" has continued to remain unchanged. Yesterday, I was getting ready to go to our last drive-in church service and I decided at the last minute to take a cup of coffee with me. Seemed simple enough. I have a full-size coffee pot, but I also have one of those one cup pots too. Since I was going to take the cup of coffee with me, I decided to use the one cup machine. I know how this coffee pot works. You put the water in the back, put your coffee of choice in the dispenser, and turn the pot on. I had decided on cream with my morning cup and I put that in my cup too. A few minutes later, I realized that I hadn't heard the machine make the "I'm working" sound. I also thought to myself, wow, good thing it didn't work, because I had forgot to put the cup under the coffee release section. So, with one swoop, I turned the machine on, and put my coffee cup where it was supposed to be. But as soon as my cup hit the spot where it was waiting for coffee to fill it, it made a splashing sound. It was sitting in coffee that had already been brewed and was now all over the counter. The coffee pot had worked. I removed my cup in an instant. It was dripping with already-brewed coffee, and when I went to set it down on the counter, I managed to spill the cream that was in the cup on the counter with the coffee that was now spreading rapidly all over the counter. I did get all the coffee and cream wiped off the counter and was able to finally get my coffee to go. All the while, I had to smile, knowing I am handling this life on the gray side with as much fun as I can. Moral of the story: just laugh at yourself because you will find out that we carry a lot of comedy material with us each day.

****

Living life on the Gray Side as the main character in the movie Groundhog Day has proven to be quite an experience. Every day different, yet the same. How can that make any sense at all? I usually walk with a friend every day because I am a social exerciser. If I have someone to talk to, I can do it; if not, not so much. Since we have had to social distance, I am trying to walk by myself. Thankfully, I take my phone with me, so I can talk to someone while I walk. I haven't had a cell phone for very long and I am not yet too savvy with it. As I finished talking to my friend, I stuck the phone in my back pocket and was almost home when I heard someone call my name. "Becky!" I looked around and waved at my neighbor's house, but I couldn't see anyone. Then I heard it again, "Becky". Okay, I stopped in the middle of the road, looking for someone who is calling my name. I wave hesitantly again; I still do not see anyone. But I hear someone saying my name. You guessed it. Yes, the phone in my back pocket was saying my name. My mom was trying to call, and somehow, I have no clue how, my phone must have connected to her call, and she was trying to get me. Now I am sure my neighbors, who are probably wondering why the neighbor lady was aimlessly waving to no one in the middle of the road, have marked me off as either being very friendly, or totally insane. Each day I am a little of both. Have a great day!

****

With all of the twists and turns of life going on around us, you will all be glad to know that over here on "The Gray Side", I am continuing to add up story after story to fill quite a few files. The story for the week:

I usually walk each day with a friend, but I realized today that I am pretty sure God has already put an exercise program in place for all of us over the age 60, whether we want one or not. I am sure most of you over that age will be able to identify with this exercise plan. For those of you like me who have 2 flights of stairs in your home, we get the extra workout plan at no extra cost. Case in point. I am in the basement; I climb the stairs, log in steps, enter the living room, log in steps, now what was I looking for? My shoes. Why am I looking for my shoes in the living room? They are always downstairs at the door where I take them off, log in steps, back down the stairs. My coat. That is what I was supposed to get when I climbed the stairs the first time. Up the stairs, log in more steps. Get the coat out of my closet, back downstairs, add more steps. Can you see The Gray Side exercise plan? No need for a gym membership, no need for a workout set at home. Heck, all you really need is The Gray Side. I am loaded with it because today I climbed my steps 4 different times just to get myself ready to walk. Who needs one of those step counters anyway? I have life on The Gray Side, and it's all I need.

****

You know you're getting old when...

I will let each of you fill in the blank as it pertains to you, but this morning I can fill it in personally: You know you're getting old when the banana you peeled for breakfast to eat with your toast is missing. My morning started out as usual. Dragging myself from a nice warm bed to meet up with a friend to walk, then returning home to have breakfast. It is not that complicated. I put a slice of toast in the toaster, peeled a banana, and waited for the water to heat for my hot chocolate. Again, not complicated. I decided to sit on the couch to eat so I could be more comfortable as I looked over our newest Bible Study. I ate the piece of toast, sipped some chocolate and went to reach for the banana. It was nowhere to be found. I looked on the floor thinking maybe I had dropped it; I looked in the kitchen thinking maybe I had left it there; I looked in the couch thinking maybe I was sitting on it. Seriously, it was nowhere to be found. Then it dawned on me. Maybe, just maybe, I already ate it and have no memory of it!!! Oh no. I think when you eat something and have no memory of it, the calories shouldn't count either. What do you think? Well, I guess I can fill in another blank to the first question, but I am still going to be on the lookout for a missing banana. The real question is: Should I eat another banana, one that I can remember???

****

166

Outdated?

For the last few days, I have been watching some of those flip it shows. You know, the ones where the house is a mess and the house flippers buy it cheap and fix it up and make a fortune. I enjoy seeing the finished product and just how they stage it to look perfect. Who lives in places like that anyway? Last night was the clincher for me, and I wasn't sure whether to laugh or cry. The Flippers were walking through their latest purchase. When they got to the bathroom, they laughed and laughed. There was a gold metal look around the shower stall; they couldn't believe it. I can tell you that 27 years ago when Paul and I built our house, they were very trendy. You guessed it. We have one. Really, how often do people change their shower stalls? Since we have had our house the bronze look was popular, the silver look came and went, dark brown was leading the style for a while and now it seems that tile is the way to go. I realized that I am officially outdated. I am pretty sure when it is time for the gold trim to be in style again, I will be in my 80's and by then, heck, I won't even be able to what color is on the stall, but I will be stylin' for sure. I also need to be careful who I let into my house. It could be a Flipper ready to take out my shower with the huge mauls they carry in their vehicles. Outdated and loving it!

****

For all you women under 40 reading this post, or any male, you might just want to pass over this story. All others, you will understand.

Today was my day to get my picture taken. Not school pictures. They used to be fun. Each year we were paraded in a line to a guy who seated us in a chair, pointed a camera at us and told us to smile. A flash of light went off, we smiled and blinked and we got back in line. Today was much different. As a matter of fact, my face never got in this photo. I am sure you guessed that today was the mammogram shoot. Oh, I have had many over the past years and I am very thankful for their accuracy. Right along with that comes a mixture of memories of past photo ops. There was the time when I was standing in a very uncomfortable position feeling like I was being smashed between two books while someone was stomping on them, and the person that put me there stepped behind a door and yelled, "Don't move." Seriously. Did she think I would sneak out while her back was turned? She must know that if I did move, I would certainly leave a part of me between the books. Not happening!!! Oh, and then they reposition you to do the same to the other side, along with the order, "Don't breathe!" I wonder if she realizes that as soon as the books come down, the breathing stops automatically. No need to be told that! But today was the best one of all. As we were finishing up, she looked at me and said the pictures are great and I did great. Yes, it was a good shoot and I am going to think what she was truly saying was that today I was very photogenic. That's my story and I am sticking to it!!!

****

Aging

I have enjoyed the ability to write on Facebook. There are times I do things in my life that are too funny not to share. I think one day I might write a book about aging, the ungraceful way. There are also days like today that remind me how many on Facebook are struggling. A granddaughter having surgery, losing a mom, a custody hearing that didn't turn out the way you planned it, a church being vandalized, a move to a nursing home, pain from a surgery a year ago, a relationship that turned sour and losing a beloved pet are just a few things that I came across today. I have to stop for a moment and ask God why? Why is there so much sadness today? Why is life so difficult? Where are You? Then I am reminded that in the book of John Jesus says, "In this world you will have trouble." Not you might have trouble, you WILL have trouble. Then He follows it by saying, "Take heart, I have overcome the world." I will never understand the "why", but I will never forget that God is good. He still sits on the throne and He will never leave us. Trust Him. Oh, and that whole getting older thing. I know my husband's birthday is July 23; I just thought it was tomorrow. That is when I planned to get him a cake and celebrate- tomorrow. Who knew today is the 23rd!!!! I am so losing it!!!!!!

****

The Class Reunion Again

This afternoon I was able to spend time with several girls that I went to school with. The smiles were everywhere, the laughter was contagious and our strength was evident. That strength did not come from lives that are perfect, but just the opposite. Some of us have experienced the loss of children, the pain of divorce, and we have struggled with health issues. Gray is becoming the color of our hair, and some of us (me) carry more pounds than we should, but we joined together today to support a friend who is facing cancer. We have all struggled in life, because life is just hard, but today for a moment we joined in prayer for our friend, a small gesture with out-of-this world returns. I thank God for the girls from school, who are now a bit older, and a lot wiser too, but best of all just plain fun!!!!! It was a great afternoon.

****

Living daily on The Gray Side

Writing for me has become somewhat fun at times. It also gives me a place to put down all the crazy things that go through my mind. That scares me. I am a mixture of crazy thinking and serious thoughts. We all are, right? So, with that in mind I invite you into my morning. Why do things always happen to me in the morning? Everyone in Barry County knows today it's snowing, the roads are questionable, and schools are closed. So, I drive anyway to the place I walk. I know you're thinking I got stuck, but I didn't. It was what happened on the way home that makes me wonder about myself! I finished walking, got in my car and started for home. I love my car. It has heated seats, heated steering wheel and a toasty warm heater. Then, I felt it. Many of you women over 50 will understand what I am going to say. It was the beginnings of that warm feeling you get right before a full-fledged hot flash hits. I am really not enjoying the heated seats at this moment, or the heated steering wheel, but they don't turn off instantly, so I had a choice to make. And if you passed me on Delton Road, you would know what my choice was. Yes, my window was rolled down and my head was as far out as I could get it and still drive. So, no, my window wasn't broken as I raced down the road. I was just feeling that cold air hit me and wondering why someone can't figure out how to have hot flashes harnessed, because I am pretty sure I could single handedly supply enough power for Delton.

****

Well, I gotta tell you the "Life on The Gary Side," swept me away today.

The malls that used to beckon me when I was younger no longer have the same appeal to me. The days of strolling through the stores, stopping at some and searching for hidden treasures on sale racks of others have come to an end. Today it was the Salvation Army Store. Oh, I have been to this store a lot, but today I realized while looking at the lady's shirts on the racks that I have arrived at shopping the "Gray Side" way. Looking intently as I searched through the clothes, I saw almost every year of my wardrobe from teen to current, right in front of me. Need a paisley shirt from the sixties? Got it. Need a dress blouse to wear under a two-piece suit? Got it! Tank tops, tee shirts, button up, no buttons, it was all there, from every decade I have lived. Oh, it was a trip down memory lane. So, when you start seeing some unique pieces of clothing on me, rest assured I am not losing it. I am reliving my youth and am identifying as a younger version of me. I am sure I will rock it! You should all join me.

****

Fun at the Car Wash

I am trying hard to get a handle on this "Life on the Gray Side'" thing, but every time I think I have a good grasp on it, it flies out of my hands into the main character of a blonde joke.

When you live in Michigan this time of the year, your car has collected melted snow, mud, and anything else that might be on our roads. My car was coated with all the above. It was time for a car wash. As I pulled into the car wash area there was one car ahead of me in line, so I knew my wait would be short! Then the driver of the car ahead of me approached my car and asked if I would back up so she could get out. I obliged. Now I was next in line. The car wash doors opened and I drove in. This is not rocket science. While the washer started up, I was focused on finding something in my purse. Then I felt it: a mist of water on my face. Hmm. I checked my window and it was up. My mind must be playing tricks on me. Did I really feel the water mist? At that moment I turned around to see that my rear driver's side window was halfway down. My car was not only getting an outside cleaning, but most of the back seat was getting cleaned too. Okay, maybe not cleaned, but it was getting wet. I guess when the lady in front of me approached my car, I must have pushed the button to open the back window too. As I parked the car and tried to wipe up a back seat full of water with a stack of fast food napkins, I realized that if laughing at oneself is healthy, I might live for a long time.

About the Author

Rebecca Hughes grew up in the 60's and 70's as the youngest child in a family of six kids. Her parents were the typical hardworking people who taught their children the value of hard work, honesty, faith and love. Married at the age of 17, she had two sons by the time she was 20 years old. She has lived in small town America her whole life, all the while collecting memories from a much simpler life. She has lived through divorce, remarriage and the reality of the empty nest and the joy of grand parenting.

She has a husband (Paul) of twenty-seven years, two married sons, seven grandchildren and two great grandchildren. She feels truly blessed.

Living her "Life on the Gray Side" has given her time to reflect on the importance of family, faith and laughter. She writes with the hope that when you read this, you too will remember a simpler time and   be encouraged, and hopefully it will make you smile.

Made in the USA
Columbia, SC
13 March 2021